Welcome

Nestled on the rugg   he
picturesque town of
breathtaking landsca
community—it is the   bles upon
this little haven.

But now Harlequin® Medical Romance™ is giving
readers the unique opportunity to visit this fictional
coastal town through our brand-new sixteen-book
continuity. Welcome to a town where the fishing boats
bob up and down in the bay, surfers wait expectantly
for the waves, friendly faces line the cobbled streets
and romance flutters on the Cornish sea breeze.

We introduce you to Penhally Bay Surgery, where you
can meet the team led by caring and commanding
Dr. Nick Tremayne. Each book will bring you an
emotional, tempting romance—from Mediterranean
heroes to a sheikh with a guarded heart. There's royal
scandal that leads to marriage for a baby's sake, and
handsome playboys are tamed by their blushing brides.
Top-notch city surgeons win adoring smiles from the
community, and little miracle babies will warm your
hearts. But that's not all....

With Penhally Bay you get double the reading
pleasure—each book also follows the life of damaged
hero Dr. Nick Tremayne. His story, a tale of lost love
and the torment of forbidden romance, will pierce
your heart. Dr. Nick's unquestionable, unrelenting skill
would leave any patient happy in the knowledge that
she's in safe hands, and is a testament to the ability
and dedication of all the staff at Penhally Bay Surgery.
Come in and meet them for yourself....

Dear Reader,

Being married to a dark-eyed, dark-haired hero of my own, I have always loved writing tall, dark and handsome heroes. Especially if they are the sort of men who know how to temper their strength and dedication with the special gentleness needed to take care of children. And if they're also wounded, in body or heart, somehow they always make me melt.

Zayed is one such hero, his own past as traumatic in its own way as the lives of the little patients he cares for. There is absolutely no room in his future for the woman whose green eyes seem to see too much of his pain.

He can tell that Emily is no ordinary woman—her dedication to their small charges is as strong as his own, but there is something special about her that sparks his reluctant awareness from their very first meeting.

It was wonderful to watch Zayed's pain and emptiness begin to fade as he worked at Emily's side, but could he ever trust her enough to let her make him whole again?

Happy reading!

Josie

SHEIKH SURGEON
CLAIMS HIS BRIDE

Josie Metcalfe

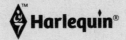

TORONTO NEW YORK LONDON
AMSTERDAM PARIS SYDNEY HAMBURG
STOCKHOLM ATHENS TOKYO MILAN MADRID
PRAGUE WARSAW BUDAPEST AUCKLAND

Recycling programs
for this product may
not exist in your area.

ISBN-13: 978-0-373-06799-2

SHEIKH SURGEON CLAIMS HIS BRIDE

First North American Publication 2011

Copyright © 2008 by Harlequin Books S.A.

Special thanks and acknowledgment are given to Caroline Anderson for her contribution to the Brides of Penhally Bay miniseries

SHEIKH SURGEON
CLAIMS HIS BRIDE

BRIDES OF PENHALLY BAY

*Devoted doctors, single fathers, a sheikh surgeon,
royalty, miracle babies and more....*

Hearts made whole in an idyllic Cornish community

**Last month Francesca and Mark tried one last time
for the baby they've always longed for...**
Their Miracle Baby by Caroline Anderson

**This month brings sexy Sheikh Zayed from his
desert kingdom to the beaches of Penhally.**
Sheikh Surgeon Claims His Bride by Josie Metcalfe

Snuggle up with dishy Dr. Tom Cornish in October
A Baby for Eve by Maggie Kingsley

A collection to treasure forever!

**These books are also available in print and
eBook formats from www.Harlequin.com**

PROLOGUE

THE pain was unrelenting, but Zayed was almost used to that by now.

What hurt his pride was to admit that, by this time in the evening, he had little chance of disguising the unevenness in his stride as he made his way down to the stretch of water-smoothed sand at the edge of Penhally Bay.

Anyway, there was nothing he could do to switch off the agony that came with the end of a busy day, other than taking large doses of analgesia, and he wasn't going to start down that path. If using those means to relieve his pain left him unfit to take care of one of his little ones, there would be no point to his existence.

He swore softly as his foot caught on the roughness of the granite steps and forced himself to concentrate a little harder. At least, at this time of an August evening, with the sun sliding towards the ocean, there were few people around to notice if he stumbled about like a drunk.

He smiled wryly at the thought, unable to remember the last time he'd tasted alcohol. It must have been back in the days when he'd been in medical school, indulging in that brief spell of belated teenage rebellion…before his world had become such a dangerous place, before everything had finally spiralled out of control.

'But Penhally isn't such a bad place to end up,' he murmured as he paused long enough to scan his surroundings, the perfect picture postcard of a Cornish fishing village. It had been only fairly recently that the influx of summer visitors drawn to the better-than-average surfing beach had expanded the place into quite a thriving little town. He'd first visited the area one summer, in his other life, and the serenity of this little place, where almost every building looked out towards the vastness of the ocean, had called to him.

Perhaps that was because it was so unlike his own country. 'Apart from the sand, of course,' he added with a half-hearted chuckle, glad that there was no one at this end of the beach to hear him talking to himself.

He leant forward to deposit his towel in the sand and the renewed stab of pain was enough to take his breath away for several seconds while he waited for it to subside.

'Stupid!' he hissed as he stripped off his cotton shirt and trousers and started the stretching routine that began every visit to the beach, knowing that it didn't matter how careful he was, by the time he finished, every nerve and muscle would be screaming for him to stop.

It was a great temptation to give in to it—it would be so much easier not to put himself through this agony. But that way his mobility and stamina would never improve, and that was unacceptable. If he didn't make the fullest recovery possible, then he wouldn't be able to help the children who needed him so badly.

Anyway, the pain was a necessary part of his life. It

was a reminder…a penance…a payment he had to make for the fact that he had survived while Leika, Kashif and so many others…

Zayed deliberately blocked the thought before it went any further. His nightmares were vivid enough without allowing himself to recall those events by day as well.

It was enough for him to know that he was guilty of having allowed them to die. The pain he felt could never be enough to balance the loss of everything he'd once held most dear.

'That is one of the good things about coming back to Penhally,' Emily murmured aloud, mesmerised by the changing colours in the streaks of cloud against the horizon while she waited for the sun to sink into the sea at the end of another perfect summer's day.

And *there* was another benefit to coming back to her home town, she added silently as a good-looking man stepped into view on the sand and proceeded to strip his clothing off.

'Oh, yes!' she breathed as the last golden rays outlined each new vista, from broad shoulders and a wide chest decorated with an intriguing swathe of dark silky looking hair to a tautly muscled belly and slim hips, all covered by darkly tanned skin. 'That is *definitely* a good reason for living near a beach.'

As she watched, he began an obviously well-practised routine of stretches before progressing to a seriously strenuous workout. For just a moment she wondered if he was putting on a show for her benefit, but there was no way that he could know she was there. This little alcove at the base of the rocks was one of the first places to be thrown into shadow as evening began to fall, and had been a favourite spot of hers ever since she'd come to live with her grandmother in her teens.

It wasn't until the man finally turned to walk into the sea that she noticed that he was limping fairly heavily, and her professional interest was raised. Had he injured himself during that punishing drill he'd just put himself through, or could the disability itself be the reason for the routine?

The light level had fallen too much by now for her to see any evidence of an injury, and while he had probably come to the beach at this time so that he could have some solitude, the idea of leaving anyone to swim alone when they might get into difficulties and need assistance wasn't something she could contemplate.

'Well, it's no hardship to sit here a bit longer,' she murmured. The air was still warm and even though a playful breeze had started up as the sun began to go down, she was perfectly sheltered where she was. Then, of course, there was the fact that she would have a second chance to look at that beautiful body when whoever he was finally emerged from the water.

In the meantime, she had some serious thinking to do and a mountain of guilt to come to terms with.

She'd been away for such a long time while she'd gone through her arduous medical training and had only realised that it had been far too long when a visit had revealed the dreadful secret her grandmother had been hiding.

'I didn't want you to come home just to watch me die, not when you had all those exams to take,' she'd explained stubbornly when Emily had arrived for a long weekend visit to give her the latest good news in person.

She'd been so looking forward to seeing Beabea's

face when she told her that she'd just been offered the plum job she'd been after at St Piran's Hospital. Admittedly, it was only a six-month placement, but she had high hopes that there might be a permanent position she could apply for at the end of that time.

The taste of triumph had turned to ashes in her mouth when she'd realised just how little time she had left with the only family she possessed in the world.

With her grandmother's permission, she'd spoken to the oncologist at St Piran's the next day, hoping against hope that there was room for some glimmer of optimism—an operation, perhaps, or chemotherapy—but, if anything, the prognosis was worse than she'd thought.

'She could have several months, but I really think it's unlikely,' the kindly man had said, leaving Emily feeling sick to her stomach. 'With this sort of thing, the patient is usually fairly well, despite the devastation going on inside, right up until the last couple of weeks. That's the point when she'll need to come into hospital or transfer into a hospice—somewhere where they'll be able to monitor the pain medication, because she'll need it by then.'

'If she's put on PCA, couldn't I take care of her at home?' Emily had pleaded, knowing just how much her grandmother loved her little cottage. The place was full of years of love and so many happy memories, and if she was put on a morphine pump for patient-controlled pain relief, Emily wouldn't have to worry that she wasn't giving her grandmother the correct dose.

'You could, initially,' he'd agreed. 'But we've found that it's often far too stressful for the patient to stay at home right to the end, knowing that their relatives are having to do so much for them and watching them die by inches. In the end, the two of you will find that you'll know when it's time to make the move, for both your sakes.'

And in the meantime, Emily had started her new job under Mr Breyley and had obtained permission to spend her off-duty hours far further away than the immediate vicinity of St Piran's.

Their little system had worked well, with Emily taking care of her grandmother's needs before she drove the hour to St Piran's, knowing that Beabea still had many friends in the Penhally area, including several in the medical profession in one capacity or another, who would be dropping in throughout the time she herself was away on duty.

And while her grandmother slept for longer stretches each day, Emily took herself off for walks along the harbour, past the Penhally Arms and the Anchor Hotel. Each time she glanced in she saw that holidaymakers and locals alike were enjoying themselves, and it seemed somehow wrong that they were oblivious of the life-and-death battle that was going on just around the corner.

A time or two she'd sat at the café on the end of the row, sipping a long frothy latte while she watched the holidaymakers leaning on the parapet of the bridge, who were watching the waters of the river Lanson hurrying on the final stretch of their journey to the sea.

She'd stood there a time or two herself, gazing down at the chuckling, purling waters tumbling over the rocks while she'd pondered on the timelessness of the view. So little had changed from the first time she'd balanced on the parapet on her stomach as a teenager, risking a painful dunking if she'd gone head first over the edge.

And yet, even though the stones and the water hadn't changed, everything else had.

She was a different person from that teenager, a doctor, now, with the job of her dreams. And her grandmother, who had always seemed so ageless that she might live for ever, was now a shrunken old lady with thin grey hair and papery skin and barely enough energy to breathe.

In fact, apart from working under Mr Breyley, which was everything she'd hoped for and more, the one bright spot in her day was if she managed to make it to the beach to complete her mind-numbing run along the hard-packed sand before her mystery man arrived.

Several times she'd been tempted to speak to him, to let him know that she was there and to get her first good look at his face, but that would have spoilt the fantasies she'd been weaving about him, especially if she found out that he was only someone she'd gone to school with.

Then there was the fact that he might see her as some sort of voyeur, hiding in the rocks while she watched him put himself through his nightly torment, but she could always counter that accusation by pointing out that she was doing nothing more than acting as an unofficial lifeguard. Not that she thought that would cut much ice with a man who seemed so driven and so utterly self-contained. In fact, his focus seemed so intense that she found it difficult to imagine that he was the sort who would ever relax enough to reveal a softer side to his nature.

'But that won't stop me imagining one,' Emily murmured as he set off into the water again lit only by the dying rays of the sun.

Today she'd really needed the distraction of watching him, to take her mind off the fact that she'd spent the afternoon settling her grandmother into her room up in the new hospice wing of the nursing home up on Penhally Heights.

The oncologist had been right after all. She'd been utterly determined to take care of her grandmother herself, even if it meant arranging to take some time off from her job. But in the end they had both agreed that it was finally time for Beabea to move out of the bedroom that had been hers ever since the day she'd moved into it as a new bride, more than fifty years ago.

'And as soon as my mystery man stops punishing himself, it will be time to go back to the cottage and get some sleep,' she told herself, although she didn't like the prospect of going back there knowing that she was going to be completely alone in the little stone cottage for the very first time.

At least she had a great job to go to in the morning, and she might hear some more gossip about that foreign surgeon who had been setting up a specialist paediatric surgical unit at St Piran's.

The buzz had been all around her ever since she'd started working for Mr Breyley at the opposite end of the dedicated paediatric block, and when she had time, she was going to take a walk upstairs to take a look at the set-up that had everybody talking. After all, paediatric surgery had been her other choice for her specialty and she hadn't finally decided which way she was going to go at the end of her six months with Mr Breyley if she *wasn't* offered the chance of a permanent post.

CHAPTER ONE

EMILY paused silently in the shadows outside the recently expanded specialist paediatric surgical unit and fell in love.

Well, she'd needed something good to happen after the shock she'd received down in her own department.

She'd barely stuck her head inside the door when Mr Breyley's secretary had beckoned her into the office.

'I'm sorry he's not here to tell you about it himself, Dr Livingston,' the rather austere-looking woman had said with a slightly frazzled glance around at the haphazard piles of paper littering her normally pristine desk. Then she had unbent enough to murmur, confidentially, 'He and his wife flew out to New Zealand this morning. Their first grandchild is on the way. He was diagnosed with transposition of the great arteries *in utero* and is arriving prematurely, so they wanted to be there for their daughter…at least, until the corrective surgery's over and done with.'

'Completely understandable,' Emily had agreed, even as panic had started to set in. Was she about to lose her job? With Mr Breyley on the other side of the world, she had lost her mentor and tutor. The hospital would be unlikely to be able to find someone of his calibre available at short notice.

Then there was the fact that it hadn't only been the job that had brought her back to Penhally. Of course, it had been a terrific step up on her career path, and the fact that it had been within easy travelling distance of Beabea had been a bonus. But now that her grandmother's condition was rapidly worsening and now she'd transferred to the hospice, the last thing Emily wanted was to have to move away, perhaps to the other end of the country for a comparable post.

She just couldn't do that. She needed to be here, in the hospital closest to Penhally, so that she could spend as much of these last precious days with her grandmother as she could. Also, there was the fact that transferring to another hospital at short notice, and so soon after starting a placement, could look bad on her CV. Anyway, there was no guarantee that she would find a comparable post either.

With the likelihood that her perfect job was going to vanish into thin air, there were other worries to be considered, too.

It was highly unlikely that the hospital would be willing to keep paying her salary until they appointed a new surgical consultant to take her on and, no matter how much she wanted to spend time with Beabea, she couldn't afford to take an expensive break, either financially or professionally.

But she had so little time left to be with her grandmother and didn't want to waste any of it travelling endless hours to and fro.

'However,' the senior consultant's secretary continued, breaking into her endlessly circling thoughts, suddenly all efficiency, 'before he left, Mr Breyley had another look at the application forms you sent in when you applied for the post on his firm. He'd remembered that you'd noted an interest in the field of paediatric orthopaedics as well, so he took your references to have a word with Mr Khalil about the situation. Anyway, he has persuaded Mr Khalil to let you join his team *pro tem*, to see whether you fit in.'

Emily blinked a bit at that. It was amazing that Mr Breyley had found time to consider her situation when he must have been desperate to start his journey to New Zealand, but she really wasn't certain that she liked the sound of his arrangements for her. It almost made her sound like some substandard piece of equipment being dumped on an unwilling recipient.

Mr Breyley was an acknowledged expert in his field and had thought her good enough to join *his* team. And considering the fact that her record throughout her training had been second to none, it was almost an insult that this Mr Khalil had needed to be persuaded to take her on, even temporarily.

'I'm sorry I can't be more specific,' the harried secretary continued, apparently oblivious to Emily's chagrin at being treated as an unwanted parcel, 'but Mr Khalil said to tell you that he'd either be in his office or in Paediatric Intensive Care.'

So here she was, on a mission to find Mr Khalil and see if she could discover why he thought *his* requirements so much higher than Mr Breyley's when he was choosing new team members.

She'd started off her search at his office and found a stunningly beautiful woman with an intriguing accent manning the desk.

'He is not available at the moment, and he will be starting his surgical list at ten this morning,' she informed Emily coolly, as kohl-lined dark eyes flicked dismissively over her from head to toe.

Emily stifled a wry grin. It was obvious that her simple summer cotton clothes had been found seriously wanting in the elegance stakes.

Well, that was just too bad. She'd long ago decided that spending half of her time in baggy surgical scrubs, with something that looked like a pair of paper knickers on her head, meant that there wasn't a lot of point in trying to impress her colleagues with anything other than her medical capabilities.

'My name is Dr Livingston,' she informed her quietly. 'I'm the new member of Mr Khalil's team and need to know where to find him as soon as possible.'

'But…you're a *woman*!' she exclaimed, and grabbed for some paperwork on the top of her immaculately tidy desk. 'We are expecting a Dr Emil Livingston, and Emil is a man's name, no?'

'Emil is a man's name, yes,' Emily agreed, almost giggling when she found herself mimicking the woman's speech patterns. There was just something about these effortlessly flawless women that rubbed her up the wrong way, probably the fact that she would have to starve herself for weeks…*months*…to wear anything like the size zero designer clothes this secretary was wearing, in spite of the fact that she tried to force herself to go for a run each day. 'But my name is Emily, with a "y", but without the corresponding chromosome.'

'Excuse me?'

Emily stifled a sigh as she glanced at her watch, forgoing any effort at an explanation of her attempt at humour.

'If you could just tell me where I can find Mr Khalil,

I would be very grateful.' It wouldn't do anything to impress her new boss if she was any later reporting for work, and she really needed to impress him if he was going to allow her to join his team properly until Mr Breyley returned from New Zealand. For Beabea's sake, she really needed this job.

'He will be up in PICU with the Hananis...the parents of a child who will have surgery this morning. I will ring him to tell him you are coming.'

'Don't bother interrupting him while he's talking,' Emily said quickly, loath to draw any extra attention to her tardiness. 'I'll find him easily enough when I get there.'

Except she hadn't found him yet.

She'd run up several flights of steps, right to the top of the hospital where the recently expanded and refurbished PICU was situated just round the corner from the brand-new surgery suite she'd caught a glimpse of when she'd come for her interview.

She'd had to knock for admittance to the ward, not privy to the code to unlock the door yet.

'I'm Dr Livingston, the new member of Mr Khalil's team,' she announced, hoping she didn't sound too winded, but taking the stairs instead of the lift was one of the habits she'd had to adopt if she was to stand a hope of keeping her weight under control.

'Welcome!' the staff nurse said with a smile as she swung the door wide. 'We had no idea we were going to be getting a woman on one of our paediatric surgical teams. I'm Jenna Stanbury.'

She, at least, had looked pleased to see her, Emily noted as she was led into the unit. Several heads looked up from what they were doing and smiled vaguely in her direction.

'I'm afraid that Tamsin…Sister Rush…has shut herself in her office with strict instructions only to be disturbed in case of fire or flood while she fights with a mountain of paperwork,' Jenna said apologetically.

'Actually, I've been trying to catch up with Mr Khalil,' she said with a grimace when she caught sight of the time on a clock shaped like a cat with a long tail swishing rhythmically to count off the seconds. At this rate she was going to be fired for poor time-keeping before she even started work.

'Don't panic,' Jenna soothed. 'The last time I saw Mr Khalil, he was going into the interview room with the Hananis to explain exactly what's going to happen during their son's operation. I sent one of the juniors in a little while ago with a tray of coffee, so you've probably got time to have a bit of a walk around while you catch your breath. Don't forget infection control procedures…he's very hot on that.'

'I'm glad to hear it,' Emily said as she reached for the gel dispenser. 'It's bad enough when an adult gets a hospital-acquired infection, but when it's a sick child…' She was pleased that her new boss was as keen on good hygiene as she was. That was one thing they had in common already.

She made her way around the unit to familiarise herself with the layout, hoping that it would soon be a second home to her. It was an environment that she felt comfortable in, where post-operative patients would be continuously supervised by batteries of monitors and their needs taken care of by highly trained specialist nurses while they began their recovery after surgery.

And there he was.

Oh, she had no idea *who* he was, just that he was the most beautiful man she'd ever seen, with thick dark hair cut short to combat an obvious tendency to curl, dark lustrous eyes with more than a hint of the exotic about them, surrounded as they were by the thickest, longest eyelashes she'd ever seen on a man. But the most beautiful thing about him was the way he was smiling as he was leaning over the equally beautiful child in an isolette, spending precious time with him while he was awake.

She watched him as he tenderly stroked an elegant, long-fingered hand over soft dark curls, smiling again as he murmured softly.

Her heart clenched at the sight of that smile and the way it lit those beautiful dark eyes from within. This was a man who loved his child and wasn't ashamed who knew it, and something inside her ached that she'd never known such unconditional love from anyone other than her grandmother.

She didn't know whether she'd made a sound or whether her presence in the doorway had finally registered on him, but suddenly *she* was the focus of those dark eyes…and they weren't smiling any more.

'Who are you? Do not come any closer,' he ordered in a voice soft enough not to startle the little child at his side, but with the obvious stamp of authority in every exotically accented syllable. 'What are you doing here? Do you wish to speak with me?'

'If you are Mr Khalil, yes, I do,' she said with a crushing sense of disappointment adding a crisp edge to the words. Where was the warm, caring father with his dark eyes full of love that she'd just lost her heart to? This man was something else entirely, the expression in his eyes almost cold enough to freeze her in her tracks in spite of the glorious Cornish summer day outside.

'And you are…?'

He was obviously a man of few words, she thought as she took his nod as permission to approach, his commanding presence growing more overwhelming the closer she came.

For the first time since she'd embarked on her medical career she actually found herself wanting to step back from a challenge, but that wasn't her way…had *never* been her way, from the day when a brusque social worker had dumped her unceremoniously on her grandmother when she'd been rescued from her parents' crushed car.

Deliberately, she straightened her shoulders and forced herself to meet that obsidian gaze, noticing for the first time that his face was marked with the evidence of deep-seated suffering, the eyes that had been so expressive such a short while ago now showing absolutely no emotion.

It took another second for her brain to compute all the other information it was receiving about the tall, lean man facing her from less than an arm's span away—the arms that were bare to the elbow in compliance with the latest infection control policy, darkly tanned skin and even darker hair on well-muscled forearms, the taut skin of his freshly-shaven cheeks, the crisp freshness of his plain white shirt startling against the natural tan of his soap-scented skin.

His collar was open, in line with the hospital's no-ties policy, and she could see a dark, delicious hollow at the base of his throat and the prominent knobs of the ends of his collar-bones and, just in the deepest part of the V of his shirt opening, a dark tangle of silky-looking hair that seemed impossibly intimate, hinting at what she might reveal if she were to reach out and unfasten more of those small white buttons.

'Well?' he said shortly, and she felt the warmth surge up into her cheeks with the realisation that for the first time in her life she'd been so busy looking at him that she'd completely forgotten to answer his question.

'I—I understand that Mr Breyley told you about me before he left for New Zealand. I'm Emily Livingston, the new member of your team,' she said, and to prove just how scrambled her brain had become in his presence, she completely forgot about infection control and held her hand out to him.

CHAPTER TWO

ZAYED blinked at the announcement that *this* was his newest colleague, so startled that he only just remembered in time not to reach for the slender hand hovering in mid-air.

One half of his brain was wondering whether anyone had remembered to tell her how strict he was about maintaining hygiene around his patients.

'You should be a *man*!' he exclaimed, while the other half of his brain busied itself with taking in the perfection of her barely sun-kissed, peaches-and-cream complexion and the blonde hair wound tidily away in an attempt to make her look professional. Then there was the lushness of her gently rounded body clad in the simplest of clothing that struck the first spark of sexual interest he'd felt in far too long.

Not that he would ever do anything about it. He couldn't.

'My secretary took down the details,' he continued, forcing both halves of his brain to work together so that his voice came out far more harshly than he'd intended.

'I know,' she said calmly, and an intriguing hint of a smile hovered at the corners of a mouth that didn't seem to have a trace of artifice deepening its soft rose colour. 'She'd left the "y" off the end of my name and added it to my chromosomes.'

He almost chuckled at the clever play on ideas, strangely delighted when he realised that there was more to this woman than met the eye, but he ruthlessly subdued the unexpected impulse. Any attraction that he felt for her would be nothing more than a momentary aberration...it could never be more than that, not since...

'Well, if "xx" is willing to work as hard as "xy", I will have no cause for complaint,' he said shortly, the old pain and the never-ending guilt gripping him anew even as he tried to banish the bitter memories from his mind.

'In that case, where do you want me to start?' she offered, and he felt a strange sense of disappointment when he saw the way she'd deliberately switched off any warmth in her expression, but what else did he expect when he'd been so cold with her?

A demanding cry behind him drew his attention before he could answer her question.

'Come and meet Abir,' he invited, and was puzzled by the arrested expression on her face, those startling green eyes of hers wide with what looked almost like surprise as they travelled from his mouth to his own eyes and back again.

He frowned, wondering what on earth was the matter with the woman as he gestured towards the child in the plastic isolette.

'He was delivered by emergency Caesarean when his mother went into full eclampsia, but there were no adverse after-effects. Both mother and child were doing well…until she noticed that his head was not like the heads of the babies of her friends.'

By this time they'd reached the isolette and he broke off to murmur a few soothing words to the fractious infant before he continued.

'Her doctor was not really sure what was the matter with the child, and there was no paediatric specialist nearby, so as she was the sister of a…friend…' he prevaricated, avoiding specifying the real connection between Abir's family and his own, 'I was asked to see the child.'

He ran his hand over the child's head, mourning the fact that all this silky dark hair would be gone in a matter of minutes now, as he was prepared for the life-changing surgery. He refused to let himself remember cradling another little head, little knowing just how short that precious life would be.

Abir had settled under his touch, his big dark eyes gazing up at the two of them with that strange solemnity that he sometimes saw in these little ones.

'If you would like to clean your hands, you could make an examination of Abir,' he invited, and stepped aside slightly to gesture towards the child, inviting Dr Emily Livingston to make her own assessment of Abir's condition.

'I used antibacterial gel on my hands just before I stepped inside the room,' she said, then startled him by blushing softly. 'And apart from trying to shake hands with you, I haven't touched anything since then.'

'So…' He repeated his gesture towards the infant, who seemed almost as captivated by the woman's blonde hair as *he* was.

'Hello, Abir. Haven't you got beautiful big brown

eyes?' she crooned as she bent down to bring her head almost to the same level as the child's. She reached out a slender hand to stroke a gentle finger over the back of a chubby little fist and smiled when the little one immediately grabbed it and held on tightly.

'That's a clever boy,' she praised as she began to stroke her other hand over the silky dark hair covering the unusually shaped skull, her voice taking on an almost sing-song quality that clearly mesmerised the child.

The tone of her voice stayed the same as she continued speaking softly to the little one so that it was a couple of seconds before Zayed realised that she was now speaking to him.

'Without seeing any X-rays, I'm assuming that this is craniosynostosis, with some of the cranial sutures fusing before birth,' she said with an air of steady confidence in her diagnosis that impressed him no end. Her fingertips were gently tracing the lines where the joins between the plates of the skull were already showing pronounced abnormal ridges. 'Is there a genetic component here—any history of Crouzon or Apert in the family, for example?'

'An uncle and a cousin,' he confirmed. 'But we only found that out when we started questioning the rest of the family. As neither of the affected members has survived, their disfigurement meant that they are rarely mentioned any more, and especially not in front of a pregnant woman.'

'For fear her baby will "catch" the problem?' she asked with a smile in the baby's direction that had him gracing her with an answering open-mouthed, gummy grin.

'That sort of superstition still lingers in some of the more remote villages in Cornwall, too,' she continued, this time smiling directly up at him as though sharing a particularly delicious secret as she added, 'At one time, it even included redheads being banned from visiting.'

'And what would be your preferred treatment modality?' He wouldn't allow himself to be beguiled by a pair of sparkling green eyes. There was no point.

'Surgery, of course, to excise the affected bone,' she answered, so promptly that he wasn't sure whether it was her own decision or one based on the fact she'd already been told about the impending surgery.

'Because?' he probed with unexpected intensity, suddenly needing her to be able to justify her assertion, although he had no idea why.

'Because otherwise the fact that the bones had already fused before he was born will mean that there's no room for expansion and his brain will end up terribly damaged. If I remember correctly, a linear craniotomy and excision of the affected sutures is most effective when performed in the first three months of life,' she added.

She was looking down into those big brown eyes, and he suddenly knew that she had recognised the gleam of intelligence already lighting them, too, and understood just what a tragedy it would be if that spark were crushed out of existence.

'What are the potential hazards of the operation?' He forced himself to ignore the sudden feeling of connection with her by concentrating on the specifics of the procedure. This was the sort of detail that he would hope she knew backwards, forwards and inside out, having taken her latest exams so recently.

There was a sudden flash of concern in her eyes, as though she was genuinely concerned that he might not be sufficiently satisfied with her answers to give her the placement on his team. But surely he'd been mistaken. She would only have been informed of Mr Breyley's departure when she'd arrived at the hospital that morning. It wasn't as if this position was one that she desperately wanted or that she'd had time to become nervous about a make-or-break interview…or was it?

There was something about the tension in her feminine frame that told him there *was* a burning need in her to gain his approval for the placement, that there was something inside her that meant she would work every bit as hard in his department as she had in his colleague's.

So, was there another reason why she wanted the job, a personal reason, completely separate from her career aspirations?

Perhaps she particularly wanted to stay in this part of the country, between the wild desolation of the moors and the rugged majesty of the coast. Perhaps she had family here, or a boyfriend she wanted to be close to.

He was almost grateful for the fact that she began speaking, able to ignore the sudden unexpected clutch of disappointment in his gut at the thought that some undeserving man had the right to wrap that beautiful body in his arms. He had absolutely no right to feel anything for this woman other than the need for her to be the best junior she could be.

'During surgery, there's the possibility of hypovolaemic shock, especially in such a young patient,' she announced with a slight quiver in her voice that belied her apparent confidence. 'There's also the chance that there might be dural tears unrecognised during the procedure that can cause cerebrospinal fluid leaks. They could leave a pathway open for infection. There could also be epidural or subdural haematoma due to surgical trauma. Post-operatively,' she continued swiftly, almost as fluently as though she were reading word for word from the relevant specialist text, 'there will be facial swelling, of course, especially around the eyes. That usually resolves in the first few weeks, but the improvement in the head shape is almost immediate.'

'And have you observed such surgery?' He was careful not to reveal just how impressed he was. Not only had she made a correct diagnosis of a relatively rare condition, but had obviously recalled, verbatim, everything she had read about it.

'Only in my teaching hospital's video library,' she admitted. 'I've always been interested in paediatric orthopaedics.'

'In that case, we just have enough time to introduce you to Abir's parents before it's time to scrub,' he announced, suddenly eager to see how well this young woman would acquit herself in an operating theatre.

As if they were obeying some invisible signal, that was the precise moment that the Hananis chose to emerge from the interview room.

Zayed led the way towards them, touched by the matched pairs of reddened eyes that were clear evidence that both parents had obviously given in to a bout of tears in his absence.

'Dr Emily Livingston, these are Abir's parents, Meera and...'

Further introductions seemed unnecessary as the

newest member of his team stepped forward to take the young mother's hands in hers.

'You have a beautiful baby,' Emily said simply, as though she'd guessed that neither of the child's parents had a detailed command of English. 'I will do everything I can to help make him well.'

Athar Hanani threw Zayed a puzzled frown, obviously needing some clarification of the situation.

'Dr Livingston will be in the operating theatre with me, assisting me while I'm operating on Abir,' he said, and when the young man switched to his own language to question the presence of a doctor who was a female, Zayed was glad that Emily couldn't understand this clear evidence of his countryman's chauvinism.

Before he could find the words to set the record straight, it was Meera who did the job for him, rounding on her husband and berating him for failing to see that the young woman doctor obviously cared about their son already.

'I put my son, Abir Hanani, in your hands,' she said to the green-eyed woman, reverting to English and wiping away the worried expression Zayed's new junior had been wearing while the sharp-edged conversation had whirled incomprehensibly around her.

'I am honoured by your trust,' Emily said, and her smile almost seemed to light up the corridor.

An hour later, Emily's concentration on the operative procedure was broken again by her conviction that Zayed Khalil was in pain.

The doctor in her had belatedly tallied the fact that there had been a slight hitch in his stride the first time he strode away from her along the corridor. At the time, she'd been full of a mixture of trepidation and excitement that she would shortly be assisting in a major surgical procedure; she'd also been slightly distracted by her sympathy for the terrified parents. It wasn't until the first time she noticed that Zayed seemed to be shuffling constantly from one foot to the other that she deliberately started to take notice.

Even as she marvelled at the fact that a live human brain was only millimetres away, under the softly gleaming dura, she found herself speculating that the handsome surgeon probably maintained his impressively fit physique by some form of vigorous exercise. Had he overdone the exercise last time? Or was the marked hitch in his stride the result of an accident in his youth—perhaps the spur that had set him on course towards his career in orthopaedics?

Suddenly, she realised that this was a very similar train of thought to one that she'd had not so very long ago; that this was the second man with impaired gait she'd met since her return to Penhally...although she could hardly say that she'd *met* the man on the beach, only ogled him from her shadowy hideaway among the rocks. Whereas Zayed Khalil...

Well, she couldn't really imagine this man standing on a beach as the last of the sunset faded around him while he pushed his body harder and harder to perform such a punishing workout. His preference would probably be some high-tech gym now that he was an important surgeon. And, besides, his position at St Piran's meant that he would have to live within a relatively short distance of the hospital. The other man definitely had to live somewhere close to Penhally, otherwise he wouldn't be able to turn up at the beach at roughly the same time each evening.

And if by some impossible fluke of coincidence they happened to be one and the same person...

Well, they aren't, and that's that, she told herself crossly as the surgeon shifted position yet again.

Afterwards, Emily told herself it was just her impatience with her silent speculation that took the brake off her tongue but, whatever it was, she couldn't believe it when she heard herself saying, 'If your back aches, you might try taking those clogs off for a while.'

There was an instant deathly hush in the operating theatre and she was certain that her mask was nowhere near large enough to hide the fiery blush that swept all the way up her throat and face until it reached her hairline under her disposable hat.

'I beg your pardon?' His eyes were almost black, as were the eyebrows that were raised so high that they nearly reached the hat covering his close-cropped hair.

In for a penny, in for a pound, she could hear her grandmother saying, and she tipped her chin up an inch before she repeated her suggestion.

'I said, if your back aches, you might try taking off your clogs and going barefoot...you could put disposable hats over your feet if you're worried about contamination.'

This time the silence seemed to stretch for ever, filled only by the rhythmic bleeps and hisses of the monitors and anaesthetic regulators.

When she was beginning to wonder if she was going to be thrown out of the theatre for breaking his concentration, he gave one swift nod.

'It is worth trying,' he said, and in an instant there

was a nurse on her knees beside him, giving a nervous giggle as she pulled a bright blue plastic hat over each of his elegant long feet before she took his theatre clogs away.

Without another word, the operation continued as seamlessly as though the last couple of minutes had never happened, the second strip of misshapen bone carefully cut out of the skull so that the prematurely fused sutures were removed entirely.

Emily was utterly absorbed in the procedure, even more so now that she was assisting than when she had merely looked at a tape.

The brutal part was over and, hopefully, would never need repeating. Now it only remained to irrigate, check for leaks and close before he'd finished. She was quite looking forward to finding out if his suturing technique was as meticulous as every other one she'd observed when he suddenly stepped back from the table.

'Taking the clogs off helped for a while,' he announced in a slightly rough-edged voice as he stripped off first one glove and then the other, somehow managing to tuck one inside the other without getting any fluids on either hand. 'But now I will watch while you complete the process.'

From the electric atmosphere in the theatre Emily knew that something momentous had just happened, but she couldn't allow it to break her concentration, not if she was going to do herself and little Abir justice.

'You might want to rest your best feature on an anaesthetist's stool while I close,' she said, as she positioned herself in his place at the table and held her hand out for the gently warmed saline, hoping her tone was matter-of-fact enough not to wound his ego. 'I'll probably take rather longer over this than you would.'

She almost chuckled when she heard Zayed murmur 'rest your best feature' in obvious amazement, and allowed herself just a couple of seconds to reflect on whether she'd spoken nothing less than the truth. The ubiquitous pale green scrubs he was wearing might be the most shapeless garments in existence, but when they were washed after every use, they soon became thin, and all it had needed was for the man to lean forward over his patient for every lean, tight curve of his muscular buttocks and thighs to be lovingly outlined.

Then it was time to switch her concentration up to full power as she thoroughly irrigated both operating fields to ensure that there were no bony fragments left inside the skull, then a minute inspection of the dura to check for any inadvertent tears. Of course, there weren't any, and the way was clear for closing the initial incisions.

'Clips or sutures?' said the voice with a delicious hint of accent even in those few words.

'I prefer sutures for areas that will be on constant show, even on a scalp where they will hopefully be covered by hair,' she explained, pausing before she inserted the first one in case he had any objections to her decision.

Although she'd been conscious that those dark eyes were watching her every move, the fact had been reassuring rather than intimidating. It had been an amazing experience to be allowed to do such a sensitive part of the procedure on her very first morning on his team. Mr Breyley had allowed her to do little more than close for weeks before he'd allowed her to lead on more routine procedures, and even then he'd hovered over her, poised to take over at the first sign that things hadn't been to his liking.

'I am sure he will thank you if he eventually goes bald,' her new mentor said dryly, and she concentrated on drawing the edges of the incisions together with as neat a row of sutures as she could manage.

'Are you happy to supervise his transfer to Intensive Care?' he asked as she positioned protective dressings over her handiwork while the anaesthetic was reversed.

'You're going to have a word with his parents?' Her quick glance in his direction told her that even sitting down for the last part of the operation hadn't relieved his pain, if the tension around his eyes was any indication. What on earth had the man done to himself?

'The waiting is awful, so I'll just let them know that the operation went well,' he explained, already on his way to the door, adding over his shoulder, 'And tell them that they'll be able to see him in PICU in—what— twenty minutes?'

'Maybe half an hour, to give us time to get him settled properly?' Emily glanced up at the experienced nurse who would be accompanying Abir on the short journey from the operating theatre to the nearby unit, and received a confirming nod.

'That will give us long enough to put some bandages on and clean his little face up a bit,' the older woman said. 'Although we're not going to be able to do anything to disguise his swollen eyes. Poor little mite looks as if he's not even going to be able to open them when he comes round.'

'Thank goodness that's one of the less important side-effects of the procedure...one that will sort itself out,' Emily murmured, even as she winced at Abir's appearance. 'But he does look as if he's gone several rounds with a prizefighter, and lost.'

After transferring him to Intensive Care she reassured herself that he was receiving the right levels of sedation and pain medication. Then there was the post-operative paperwork to take care of, so it was nearly an hour before she was able to think about the sudden detour her career had taken. And as for finding time to hunt down a cup of coffee and something to put in her rumbling stomach...

'Forget it,' she muttered as she hurried towards the outpatients clinic in response to her first bleep.

'Mr Khalil has been called down to Accident and Emergency, and he is very particular about his clinics starting on time,' snapped the heavily accented voice of his disapproving secretary. 'Some of his patients have travelled a very long way to see him.'

Unspoken, but hovering in the air like a bad smell, were the words 'and they won't be happy to see some-one as insignificant as *you* when they walk in the room', but there was nothing Emily could do about that. All she could do was dive in at the deep end and hope that she didn't drown before he arrived.

Her heart nearly stopped when she stuck her head round the doorway to the waiting area and realised that the majority of the people waiting there were proba-bly going to have as little command of English as the Hananis.

'Don't panic,' said a reassuringly Cornish voice be-hind her. 'I've put out the call for an interpreter, just in case.'

'Were my thoughts *that* obvious?' Emily asked as

she turned to find a pair of dark eyes smiling up at her from a motherly body in a uniform that could have done with being a size larger.

'Not your thoughts, maid, but the look on your face told me you were about to head for the nearest hidey-hole.' She chuckled richly. 'So, shall we make a start? I'm Keren Sandercock, by the way.'

'I'm very pleased to meet you. As you've probably gathered, I'm Emily Livingston, the newest member of Mr Khalil's firm.' She gulped. 'I know it will slow everything down, but could you possibly give me a couple of minutes with each file before you show the patient in?' she suggested.

'I can do better than that,' Keren said with a smile. 'I can introduce you to each of the patients and tell you all about them. Save you all that time trying to decipher the notes.' She winked slyly. 'He might be the most wonderful surgeon and the best looking man at St Piran's but his writing's atrocious. And anyway, I've been part of this unit ever since Mr Khalil set it up so I've already met them all.'

'What do you mean, *he set it up*?' Emily hurried in her wake and found herself obeying instantly when Keren pointed briskly at the gel dispenser.

'You mean you've joined the madhouse without knowing anything about what's going on here? You'm brave, maid.' She chuckled richly again and hitched one ample hip on the corner of a desk that was already groaning under a mountainous pile of files. 'Well, here's the potted version. Mr Khalil was given permission to set up this paediatric orthopaedic unit on the understanding that he is free to treat children from his own country who would otherwise not be able to get any help. Of course, he also treats patients from the area around St Piran's, but his special interest is the ones who wouldn't have a hope of getting any surgery if he didn't bring them over here.'

Emily was speechless, but before she could find the words to ask how she hadn't heard a word about what was going on here, there was a brisk tap at the door.

'Why are you not started?' demanded a heavily accented voice, and Emily didn't need to turn round to know exactly who had just marched into the room, neither did she need to see the sour expression on Keren's face to know that the other woman shared her feelings about Zayed Khalil's secretary.

Start as you mean to go on, she could hear her grandmother's voice advising her when she began each new project, and she whirled sharply to face the intruder.

'Out!' she ordered firmly, flinging one hand out with a finger pointing directly at the door. 'And you will *never* come into my room again without waiting to be invited. Is that clear?'

'It is not *your* room,' she sneered. 'It is *Zayed's* room. *He* is the consultant.'

'And that is all the more reason why a *secretary* should never enter without an invitation,' Emily insisted. 'What goes on in this room is private and confidential and you will *not* walk in again like that or I will report your unprofessional conduct to Mr Khalil. So, unless you have brought me some important paperwork pertaining to one of the patients waiting outside, anything you have to say to me can be communicated by telephone. Please, leave. Now.'

'Good for you, maid,' Keren murmured as the elegant fashion plate flounced out of the room, shutting the door sharply in her wake as she no doubt muttered imprecations through clenched teeth. 'She needed telling, but I'm afraid you've made yourself an enemy there, especially as she's angling to marry our gorgeous consultant.'

Emily's instant pang of dismay was followed by a silent admission that the two of them would look perfect together, tall and dark-haired with the same deep gold skin...

For heaven's sake! What did it matter what he did in his private life? She had a roomful of patients to see.

'Well, now that we've got rid of her, perhaps we should start on the clinic,' Keren continued briskly as she picked the top file off the pile. 'We're a couple of minutes early, but I can't see any of them complaining about that. Now, your first customer is Ameera Khan. She's here for her final check-up before she returns home. Her operation was fairly simple and straightforward—the correction of a break which had gone untreated and had set badly, leaving her with limited movement in her right arm.'

Emily tipped the X-rays out of the accompanying envelope and slid the first set under the clips at the top of the view box. She winced when she saw the way the original break had healed so that virtually no rotational movement had been possible. The second set had obviously been taken shortly after surgery had been completed, with plates and screws much in evidence to hold everything back in the correct position while it healed. The final set had that morning's date printed at the top and showed good progression in the healing process.

Meanwhile, Keren had flipped open the file and when the first thing Emily saw was a set of photographs of a solemn-eyed child cradling her twisted arm with a hopeless expression on her face, she could understand exactly why her new boss had been determined to help.

'Can you show Ameera in?' she asked while she scanned the notes as quickly as she could, looking for any problems that might have been noted at the time of the operation. There was nothing untoward—in fact, this was the sort of simple problem that should never have necessitated a child having to travel to a strange country for treatment…unless her own was so impoverished that even the most basic facilities were unavailable.

The little girl who came bouncing in through the door looked nothing like the sad-eyed waif in the photos, and the young woman who accompanied her was having trouble keeping up with her, especially as she was heavily pregnant.

'This is Mrs Khan,' Keren began the introductions. 'And this is Dr Emily Livingston, who is working with Mr Khalil. She would love to see how strong and straight your arm is, Ameera.'

The interpreter had slipped into the room almost unseen behind the woman and child and, as Keren spoke, translated her words into a mixture of incomprehensible sounds that sounded almost like spoken music.

Without any hesitation, the little girl tugged her sleeve up to reveal a scar so neat that, in time, it would probably become almost unnoticeable.

It didn't take long for Emily to gain her trust, especially when she discovered that the youngster was ticklish, and it was very satisfying to note that every test she performed confirmed that the prognosis was excellent.

'It is good, yes?' her mother asked, clearly worried about her daughter.

'Yes. It is good,' Emily confirmed with a broad smile. The flaking skin that was the result of the time spent in a cast would soon disappear, and the way Ameera eagerly completed every task Emily had set her spoke well for her regaining her full range of motion in time, even if structured physiotherapy wouldn't be available once she returned to her own country. 'I just wish I could take another photo to put in the file.'

'But you can!' Keren exclaimed as she hurried across to a cupboard at the other side of the room. 'I'm sorry, but I completely forgot to give you the camera.'

'Ah!' the little girl exclaimed when she saw what Keren was fetching. She obviously knew what was expected of her and pulled her sleeve up again, this time proudly showing off her straight arm with a broad smile.

'Thank you so much,' her mother said, her dark eyes glittering with the threat of happy tears. 'Everybody. Thank you so much for Ameera arm.'

'You'd better go away before you make us all cry,' Keren said, and when the interpreter translated what she'd said, everybody gave a watery laugh.

'It's a good job I didn't have time to put any mascara on after my shower,' Emily muttered wryly after the door closed behind them. 'If they're all going to be like that one, I'd have ended up with a bad case of panda eyes.'

'Maid, that's why mine is waterproof,' Keren confided. 'If it isn't the successes like Ameera tugging at your heartstrings when you see them put right, it's the parents arriving with their kids, terrified that no one's going to be able to do anything to help.'

Emily suggested that she show the next patient in, suddenly conscious that being close to Beabea wasn't the only reason why she wanted Zayed Khalil to confirm her position on his team.

In little more than half a day she'd been allowed to assist in an operation that would change a tiny child's life expectation and had seen a little girl's hopeless expression change to one filled with the joys of being alive. And neither would have been possible without the unit to which she was now attached, and the man whose determination had driven its inception.

CHAPTER THREE

She'd been wrong about the hair on his chest, she thought as she drove towards Penhally that evening, grateful that she hadn't been asked to be on duty this evening.

She hoped that Mr Breyley had explained the special circumstances that had led him to absolve her from staying within easy reach of the hospital while her grandmother was so ill, but she certainly hadn't felt up to discussing the matter with her new boss—at least, not until she'd sorted her head out and relegated her crazy awareness of the man to its proper place.

A blush heated her cheeks at the realisation that she'd actually been…what was the current term?…checking her new boss out while he'd been bending over Abir's head on the operating table.

That was something she'd never done before, never been interested in doing, if the truth be told, but when Zayed Khalil had leant forward over Abir and the V of his top had gaped forward…

'Well, I could hardly help seeing, unless I closed my eyes,' she muttered defensively, and even that wouldn't have erased the image once it had been imprinted on her retinas.

She'd wondered about his chest when she'd seen the hint of dark hair at the opening of his shirt, and had speculated about the amount of body hair he would display if she were ever to see him naked.

'Well, it certainly isn't a mean scattering of wiry hairs,' she said with a strange sense of satisfaction, even as her body sizzled with heat at the idea of seeing the man totally naked. Mean was the last word she would use to describe the thick, dark pelt that had covered him as far as she could see down the front of his scrub top. As for whether it was wiry… She snorted aloud at the thought that she might ever have the opportunity to find out.

'As if!' she scoffed at the idea of ever becoming familiar enough with the man to run her fingers over the dark swells of his pectorals, trailing them through the thick silky-looking strands until she found the flat coppery discs of his male nipples and—

'Enough!' she snapped into the privacy of her little car, and leant forward to flick the radio on, loudly. 'The last thing I need is to arrive at the home looking all hot and bothered.' Her grandmother may be just weeks away from the end of her life but she certainly hadn't lost her keen eyesight or her unfailing instinct for when there was something on Emily's mind.

'So, how's the job going?' Beabea asked, almost before Emily had settled into the chair beside her bed. 'Are you still enjoying it as much as you thought you would?'

Emily smiled wryly at the fact that her grandmother had picked the one topic that she would rather not have talked about, at least until she'd banished those strange new feelings of awareness that were plaguing her.

'By the time I got to work this morning, Mr Breyley was on his way to New Zealand,' she announced, hoping that the ramifications of her side-tracked job would fill the time until Beabea's next round of medication made her too drowsy to pick up anything untoward.

The story of the consultant's concerned dash to the other side of the world so that he and his wife could be there for their daughter and new grandchild was like meat and drink to a woman who knew almost everything that happened within a fifty-mile radius of Penhally. It was testimony to the fogging effect of the analgesics that it was some time later before she suddenly realised what a disastrous effect it might have on her granddaughter's employment.

'But your job!' she exclaimed breathlessly. 'If he's gone away, does this mean that you're going to have to move away? Oh, Emily! And you've only just moved back, and I was so enjoying being able to see you each day...'

'Hush, Beabea, it's not a problem,' she soothed, squeezing her grandmother's hand gently, almost afraid that she might shatter the delicate bones. 'Before he left, Mr Breyley organised another job for me in the interim, until he comes back.'

'What sort of job? There can't be two posts for the same work, surely?' She was still fretting.

'Not exactly the same, no,' Emily conceded. 'But I've certainly fallen on my feet with the new post. It's paediatric orthopaedics and I went into Theatre this morning and the consultant actually let me assist.'

'On your first day in the job?' Beabea was understandably amazed. She'd had to listen patiently at the beginning of Emily's time on Mr Breyley's firm while she had moaned about wanting to do more than observe and do endless paperwork and legwork.

'On my very first day,' she agreed with a triumphant grin. 'It was an operation on a little boy. The bones of his skull had fused too soon and we had to—'

'Don't tell me any of the gory stuff,' Beabea warned with a grimace. 'I don't like thinking about it when it's happening to little ones. It's bad enough when it's adults. At least they can understand what's happening and why.'

'Softy,' Emily teased. 'But I know what you mean. I hate the idea that they'll be in pain so I always double-check their medication.'

'But you say this new man let you assist. Does that mean passing the tools or instruments or whatever they're called, or—'

'No. There's a member of theatre staff who does that. I was allowed to irrigate the incision—'

'Irrigate? That sounds like something I'd do in the garden,' Beabea teased, and Emily's heart lifted that she was in good enough spirits to joke.

'Then I stitched everything up and put the dressings on before he was transferred to Intensive Care.'

'And what did the consultant think of your work?' Beabea quizzed, and Emily felt the swift tide of heat flood into her cheeks. She was so grateful that there was a knock at the door before she could find an answer that wouldn't reveal her own thoughts about the consultant.

'Am I intruding?' said an unexpected male voice, and a greying head appeared round the edge of the door.

'Dr Tremayne!' Beabea exclaimed, and Emily was amused that her grandmother sounded almost flustered. Well, for an older man he wasn't bad looking, she sup-

posed, and for a woman of her grandmother's genera-
tion, the idea of a good-looking younger man seeing her
in her bed was probably plenty of reason for embarrassment.

'I was just visiting a couple of patients and thought
I'd call in on one of my favourite ladies—unless it's in-
convenient. I can always come back another time.'

'Not at all!' Beabea exclaimed, her cheeks several shades pinker. 'Emily, can you get another chair
for Dr Tremayne? This is my granddaughter, Emily
Livingston—*Dr* Emily Livingston,' she amended with
evident pride. 'She's working at St Piran's.'

'Is she now?' His dark brown eyes twinkled at Emily
but didn't cause so much as a twinge of reaction. 'She
hardly looks old enough and definitely looks far too
pretty to toil away in a hospital. Are you sure you aren't
harbouring a longing to train as a GP and move back to
Penhally?'

'There isn't a lot of call for paediatric orthopaedic
surgery in Penhally,' she pointed out politely. 'And I'm
thoroughly enjoying working with Mr Khalil in the unit
he's set up to operate on the children he flies in from
his own country.'

Uh-oh! she thought as she saw the distinct spark of
interest in her grandmother's eyes. She had definitely
said far more than she'd intended, and it was time to
beat a hasty retreat before she was subjected to an em-
barrassing grilling in front of the GP.

She stood up and gestured towards the chair she'd
been using. 'If you'll excuse me, I'll just go and see if
there's any possibility of an extra cup of tea while you
talk to my grandmother.'

'There's no need to leave on my account,' he began,

but she made her escape and hurried down the corridor, suddenly overwhelmed anew by the significance of the GP's visit.

It had been bad enough when she had been taking care of Beabea in her little cottage. But at least there, any professional medical visits from Dr Tremayne and the health visitors and nurses had taken place while she had been at work. Any adjustments to her medication had already been made by the time she'd returned.

Nick Tremayne was obviously a caring doctor who was concerned enough about his elderly patient to visit frequently and spend time making sure she was comfortable, but to actually be in the room while they discussed her worsening pain and, God forbid, speculated on how much worse it would get, was more than Emily could deal with.

This was her grandmother, the last member of her family left alive. Once she was gone, Emily would be totally alone in the world and she didn't think she could cope with talking about how little time there was left.

'I'm not really thirsty, dear,' Beabea said when she returned with a little tray, and her voice bore the slurring that told Emily that she'd received a recent boost of medication. 'I'm feeling quite tired. Perhaps I'll have a little sleep. Thank you for coming, Doctor. I'll see you... see you...'

Emily felt the threat of tears burning her eyes.

Not so long ago, Beabea would have been impatiently waiting for the man to go so that she could ask endless questions about the interesting situation her granddaughter had skated over earlier. It was a measure of the rapid progression of the disease that all she'd wanted to do was drift off to sleep.

'I promise we'll do our best to keep her discomfort to a minimum,' Nick Tremayne reassured her quietly. 'We pride ourselves on making a dreadful situation as easy as possible for both patient and family, but if you have any concerns or need to speak to me at any time…'

'Thank you,' she whispered, 'but nothing can really make it any easier when you're losing the only person in the world who…' Her throat closed up completely and she was unable to utter another sound.

To her utter mortification, the tears started to stream down her cheeks and with one last despairing look at the precious figure slumped against the mountain of pillows, she fled from the room.

It wasn't very far from the front door of the nursing home to the steps from Mevagissey Road down onto the beach and Emily made it at a flat-out run, uncaring for once whether anyone saw her tear-stained cheeks or not.

Once on the beach, she kicked off her shoes and made for the hard-packed sand at the water's edge, knowing that she desperately needed the physical exertion of a long run to get herself under control again.

There were still a number of surfers taking advantage of the waves ramped up by the evening's onshore wind, but they seemed every bit as oblivious to her presence as she was to theirs once she hit her stride.

She had no idea how long she pounded backwards and forwards, but eventually the fact that her legs were shaking with a combination of exhaustion and lack of food slowed her pace and forced her to take refuge in her usual spot among the rocks at the base of the cliff.

Almost before she'd settled herself into her little haven she caught sight of her mystery man making his

way to his usual spot, as if he'd been waiting for everybody to leave the foreshore.

As on every other occasion, he began with a series
of stretches and warm-up exercises before he started to
push himself further and harder than ever.

Even in the depths of her own misery Emily could
see that there was something different this time. It was
almost as though he couldn't find his usual rhythm, or
perhaps the injury that had given him the limp was more
painful than usual. Whatever it was, she could tell that
he was struggling, but she had a feeling that he was so
stubborn that he would be more likely to do himself
further damage than give in to the disability, no matter
how temporary it was.

The harder he tried the more concerned she became,
until all her concentration was on what he was doing
rather than on the misery that had driven her down to
the beach so precipitately.

Even as she watched, he faltered and nearly fell, only
just managing to stay on his feet, then, with a despairing shout towards the last of the sunset he sank to the
sand.

For several minutes he sat hunched over, the very picture of disheartened male ego. She felt so sorry that all
his efforts over the last few days seemed to have been
for nothing, and for the sake of that dented ego would
happily have remained out of sight if he'd simply left
the beach when he'd recovered.

As it was, she was still watching him when he gathered up his belongings, but when he went to straighten
up, something went wrong and he virtually collapsed
onto the sand again with a hoarse cry.

'Dammit, what have you done to yourself now?' she

demanded under her breath. One half of her wanted to hurry across to offer her help, but she was almost certain it would be refused—there weren't many men who would willingly accept physical assistance from a woman.

So she stayed where she was, her gaze riveted to him as she waited for him to make a successful attempt at getting to his feet.

Only it didn't happen, even though he tried twice more.

'Enough is enough,' she growled when he started to make a third attempt, even though she could see clearly that he must be suffering from some sort of muscular spasm in his back or his leg. She snatched a quick breath for courage, hoping that whoever it was would have the sense to accept the helping hand she was about to offer.

'Hang on a minute,' she called as she stepped out from the shadows at the base of the cliff. 'Let me give you a bit of support so you don't hurt yourself any further.'

She broke into a jog and arrived at the man's side just as he turned to look up at her from his crumpled position on the sand.

'Zayed! I mean Mr Khalil,' she hastily corrected herself when she recognised his unmistakable face in spite of the encroaching dusk.

'What are *you* doing here?' he snapped, for all the world like a trapped and wounded beast.

Emily recoiled from his harsh tone, but she'd suffered much worse from patients during her training and survived.

'I live not far away, in one of the cottages in the old part of Penhally,' she explained simply, sticking to plain facts. 'I was visiting my grandmother and came for a run on the beach.'

His frown was disbelieving until his eyes dropped to her bare feet and the sand-encrusted hems of her trousers.

'In that case, if you have finished your run, you can go home to your cottage and leave me in peace.'

'To leave you sitting on the beach all night in pain?' she challenged. 'I don't think so. If you remember, I've taken the Hippocratic oath, too. Now, where does it hurt? What have you done to yourself?'

He stayed stubbornly silent for such a long time that Emily began to think that he really was going to refuse her help.

Finally, when there was so little light remaining that it was only the paleness of the silvery sand that showed her where he was, he cleared his throat.

'I have had reconstructive surgery after an injury,' he admitted in a voice that clearly contained disgust at his own weakness.

It was very easy for Emily to read between the lines, especially since she'd seen the stubborn way he'd been determined to struggle on in Theatre that day.

'And at a guess, you've been pushing yourself to get fit on top of days filled with a punishing regime of surgery and assessments as well as late nights and early mornings in Intensive Care.' She shook her head in disbelief at what he'd been putting himself through, before realising that he wouldn't be able to see it. 'You were already hurting earlier on today. What on earth made you think you were in a fit state to come down here and push yourself like this?'

Without giving herself time to think about the advisability of what she was doing, she stepped behind him and knelt in the sand to put one hand on each of his shoulders.

'Where is the pain worst?' she demanded, refusing to let herself think about the warmth of his oiled-satin skin as she ran both thumbs up his neck, one on each side of his cervical vertebrae.

Emily could feel the tension in every one of his muscles, but whether that was as the result of the pain or because she was touching him she didn't know. All she knew was that she needed to help him if she could… and if he would let her.

'Relax,' she urged as she began to gently massage the knotted muscles at the base of his skull. 'Is it too painful to bend your knees up and rest your forehead on them?'

Relax?

Zayed stifled a groan as he contemplated his alternatives: humiliate himself by attempting to crawl off the beach on his hands and knees or pillowing his head on his stacked forearms and letting her continue.

Didn't the woman know she was asking for the impossible? He hadn't been relaxed since he'd looked up from Abir's bedside and seen her standing in the doorway.

She'd been like a ray of sunshine with her blonde hair and pale summery clothes sprinkled with flowers, and as for those eyes…their limpid green had seemed cool and soothing as they'd taken his measure across the room, even as they'd sparked something impossible deep inside him.

Impossible?

Yes, he reminded himself bitterly.

She was nothing like Zuleika, and even if she had been, he was not free to do anything about this unwelcome attraction. He would never be free of the guilt.

'It is not necessary,' he argued brusquely, hating the weakness that made this unavoidable, then gave in to the inevitable and settled his head on his arms.

'Yes, it is,' she countered, 'unless you're prepared to spend the night on the beach. And the local police will be around in a while on their patrol to check for drunken kids, and worse.'

'Worse?' he repeated, hazily aware that his brain function appeared to be strangely sluggish. All he seemed to be able to concentrate on was the musical sound of her voice, the light floral scent that was swirled around him by the sea breeze and the fact that she was touching him as if she actually cared about his pain.

'Drugs,' she said, and for a moment he couldn't remember what they'd been talking about.

Was she recommending analgesia for his pain or...?

'In some of Cornwall's coastal towns it's quite common, particularly during the summer holidays,' she continued, even as he was still trying to marshal all the reasons why blunting his physical and mental responses wasn't a good idea. 'So far, Penhally seems to have escaped, but that's probably because, in spite of the influx of holidaymakers each year, it's essentially the same close-knit community it's always been, with everyone looking out for each other...and keeping an eye on each other.'

He agreed with her assessment of the special charm of Penhally and its inhabitants. It was a major reason why, when he'd decided to set up a unit dedicated to the less fortunate of his little people, he'd wanted it to be close to this area. And when the big house up on the cliff had become available...

Ah, it was so hard to follow a single train of thought. The things she was doing to his muscles with those clever fingers, searching out each knot in turn and concentrating on it until it finally loosened. It almost seemed as if she had magic in her hands so that, for the first time since he'd rejected the mind-numbing effects of the analgesics his surgeons had prescribed, he was free of the gnawing pain.

'What happened?' she asked, her voice so soft that it was barely audible over the rhythmic susurration of the waves over the sand.

Immediately, he felt himself grow tense.

There was no way that he could tell this woman about the violence and destruction that had resulted in his injuries. For all that she was a professional woman, there was something essentially innocent about her that would probably be destroyed if she were to hear of the chaos and misery that he had brought down on his family and friends.

'I'm not asking what caused your original injury,' she hurried to add, almost as if she was able to read his reluctance through her fingertips. 'I meant, what happened today to set this off? You're not usually this bad.'

'How do you know I am not always like this?' he asked, grateful that she wasn't trying to pry. 'We only met for the first time this morning. Perhaps I am always this crippled.'

It was her turn to tense up, her fingers ceasing their painful but ultimately soothing ministrations.

He heard her mutter something under her breath but before he could summon up the energy to turn and face her she began speaking.

'It's true that we met this morning when I came to the unit for the first time, but…well, I've seen you before, several times. Here, on the beach.'

The final words emerged in a rush, as though there was something shameful about them. He shook his head. It was more likely that she was making things up for some reason of her own.

'That is impossible. I never come down here until the beach is empty. I deliberately leave it until the light is fading, but I would have seen you.'

'Not when I'm sitting in the shadows at the base of the cliff,' she said firmly, her fingers taking up their rhythm again. 'There's a place in between the jumble of rocks behind us where I used to come as a child…my thinking place, I used to call it. I discovered it shortly after I came to live with my grandmother.'

'So, while I have been thinking I have the beach to myself, you have been…' He paused, tempted to say spying, but that was a harsh word for someone who'd accidentally ended up sharing a public space.

'I've been watching over you, I suppose,' she confessed, sounding rather uncomfortable about making the admission.

'Watching over me?' He hadn't needed anyone to do that since he'd moved to Cornwall. It had only been in Xandar that he'd had to be surrounded by armed security. And even then it hadn't prevented the dissidents from…

'Surely you realise how dangerous it can be to swim alone,' she rebuked him sternly. 'Especially when you've been pushing your body the way you do. And to do it in the dark is just asking for trouble. If you got cramp, or—'

'So you appointed yourself my unofficial lifeguard,' he said wryly, not quite certain how he felt about the idea, or about the fact that she hadn't said something about it sooner. After all, they'd been working together for most of the day. Surely she could have said something about seeing him on the beach at Penhally.

'Actually, I didn't know who you were until a few minutes ago,' she admitted, much to his surprise. 'Because you only ever came down here at sunset, you were always silhouetted against the sky, so I never saw your face.'

'But, when you saw me at St Piran's…'

'If you'd taken your clothes off, I might have recognised you,' she joked, but the image her words planted in his head made their present situation seem far too intimate, with her hands touching his naked back.

And he didn't even have the option of walking away from her because he wasn't yet certain that he could make it to his feet unaided.

'So, what *did* happen today to get your back in such a painful mess, unless…does it just do this every so often without provocation?' she asked, returning to her question, and he grabbed the topic like a drowning man grabbing a lifeline.

'There was provocation,' he said wryly. 'I made the mistake of picking one of the patients up.'

'But you do that all the time.' She sounded puzzled. 'I've seen you, when you're examining them. You don't just ask the parents to put them on the couch and examine them like a bug under a microscope—you make friends with them and put them at their ease.'

'Until I forgot to take my mask off and the patient panicked,' he told her, while a strange feeling of warmth spread through him at the approval he heard in her voice. 'He fought me and I nearly dropped him—'

'And overloaded your back,' she finished for him. 'No wonder it was killing you while you were operating on Abir. You should have rescheduled the surgery until you'd recovered.'

As if anything was that easy.

He suddenly realised that he'd been sitting there for far too long, lazing like an overfed cat while his responsibilities piled up around him, responsibilities that someone as happy-go-lucky as Emily Livingston couldn't possibly understand. She probably didn't have anything more pressing on her mind than picking up the threads of the social life she'd left behind when she'd left Penhally to go to medical school.

He grabbed his scant belongings and surged to his feet, amazed that he was actually able to do it without the vicious stab of agony that usually accompanied such precipitate activity.

'Would you have wanted to be the one to tell Meera and Athar Hanani that the surgery they had been steeling themselves for—the nightmare of having the head of their baby son cut open and part of his skull removed—was not going to happen today because the surgeon had a pain in his back?'

'Oh, but I didn't mean—'

'Go back to your cosy little cottage, Dr Livingston,' he interrupted rudely as anger froze all the soft warmth that spending time with this woman had created. 'I will not be requiring your self-imposed offices as lifeguard tonight, so you can leave with your conscience clear.'

As he strode away from her he heard a brief sound of distress carried on the salty breeze but deliberately ignored it, ignored, too, the manners that had been drilled into him from infancy that demanded he should thank her for what she had tried to do for him.

He couldn't permit himself to register the fact that for the first time since the explosion his stride was almost perfectly even, or that the warmth of her hands seemed to linger in every cell of his back under the shirt he'd tugged on over his head.

All he could allow himself to think was that he should have known that someone who looked as beautiful as she did couldn't possibly understand the imperatives of duty and responsibility that were the only way he could assuage the crushing guilt he bore.

In fact, someone like Emily was the last person he needed in his life or on his team. She had been a distraction today, with her soft blonde hair and sparkling green eyes, her womanly body and her ready smile, and he couldn't afford any distractions.

'She will have to go,' he said firmly, startling a couple perusing the menu outside the door of the Anchor Hotel. He could feel their concerned eyes boring into his back for several moments as he continued past the parade of shops towards the promontory where the lifeboat station dominated that side of the bay.

'I will call her into my office and tell her that it would be better if she looked for a position in her original specialty,' he muttered as he passed Penhally Bay Surgery and Althorp's boatyard, and had to fight down a pang of remorse that he wouldn't get to watch her fledgling but meticulous surgical technique again.

He'd been so impressed when she'd apparently stepped up to the table without a trace of nerves, in spite of the fact that her involvement in the surgery had come completely out of the blue. She was good, and with the right guidance, had the potential to be excellent. It was a shame that...

That what? he challenged himself as he finally reached his car. That she was too beautiful and he was too susceptible? That certainly wasn't her fault. And neither was the fact that he'd just jumped down her throat for suggesting that he hadn't been in a fit state to perform Abir's surgery.

She was probably right, but he'd grown so accustomed to working through the pain that he just hadn't realised how bad it was going to get until he had already been in trouble.

He swore viciously under his breath when he finally admitted that he wasn't going to enjoy what he was going to have to do in the morning, glad that since he was using his own language there was almost no likelihood that anyone would be able to understand him.

CHAPTER FOUR

'You're from Penhally, aren't you?' asked Nance Penwarden, one of the newer members of staff recruited to the unit who almost seemed to have been waiting for her to step inside the door the next morning.

She was an older woman, who had returned to nursing as a way of supporting herself and her children after the breakdown of her marriage.

'I grew up there, but I've only just returned after going away to train,' Emily confirmed. 'Why do you ask?'

'Oh, it's just that we had one of the Penhally GPs in this morning—Dr Tremayne? He called in to see one of his patients who had to come in to our unit after emergency surgery as a result of an accident on the family farm—his pelvis was fractured and had to be stabilised,' she added briefly, before hurrying on. 'Dr Tremayne stayed with the parents for a while, explaining everything and calming them down, then he asked me to show him around the unit and he ended up spending some time talking to some of our older children.'

Her smile was slightly embarrassed and Emily suddenly wondered if one of the reasons why she'd returned

o such a demanding profession had been the possibility of looking for a replacement for her husband.

'He was really good with them, really patient,' she continued. 'He spent ages answering questions and… well, you wouldn't happen to know if he's married, would you?' she asked in a sudden rush, and Emily's suspicion was largely confirmed.

'He was married and has several children…three, I think, and all grown up…but I'm almost certain that he's a widower now.' Emily had heard a rumour going around Penhally about some sort of a connection between Nick Tremayne and Kate Althorp, but she wasn't one to spread gossip. Neither did she really have time for this conversation when there were patients to see, and especially with Zayed stalking towards her with a steely expression on his face.

'Dr Livingston, would you come into my office, please,' Zayed said, with a rough edge to his voice that had Emily wondering whether he'd had as little sleep as she had, last night.

'Certainly, Mr Khalil,' she replied formally and stepped away from the side of Abir's cot, pausing only to give Meera a reassuring smile as she left the room.

In his long-legged wake she only had time to throw glance at the pile of files with which she'd been hopi to familiarise herself this morning. With the outpati and referral clinics yesterday, to say nothing of surgery, she hadn't really had much time to tak specifics of each of the unit's little charges.

That was why she'd driven in to St Piran' of hours before her shift was due to start, hadn't arrived before the man who had

most every one of her thoughts for the last twen
hours.

No, actually it had been far longer than that, she
alised as she followed him along the brightly decora,
corridor towards his office. She hadn't recognised it .
the time, but it had been in his persona as the intensely
focused man on the beach that he'd first set her hormones humming.

That had been a first for her.

She'd never believed that she was so shallow that
she would allow a muscular body or a handsome face
to dictate her attraction to a man. But Zayed had that,
and more—a keen intellect, a caring heart and a sense
of responsibility that...

Oh, who was she trying to kid? It hadn't been his
intellect that she'd been dreaming about so heatedly. It
had been the feel of his skin under her hands, the way
the swells and curves of his hard-won muscles had filled
her palms and the subtle smell of musk that had lingered
even after she'd made her way to Beabea's cottage.

'Take a seat, please,' he demanded quietly, drag-
ging her instantly away from her mental images of the
bronzed figure silhouetted against the sunset to the professional man in front of her.

Not that it completely drove the thoughts away. How
could it when she could see the same lean, powerful
body, albeit this time clothed in pale coffee-coloured
trousers and a dark bronze shirt that brought out unexpected gleams of gold in those beautiful dark eyes?

His face was every bit as handsome as the first time
he'd seen it, but after watching it at intervals for the
st twenty-four hours she felt as if she was actually
tting to read some of the emotions that were going

on behind the 'official' look he seemed to hide behind
sometimes.

There was something about his expression this morning that she hadn't seen before…an uneasiness that sent
warning prickles up the back of her neck, especially
when he couldn't seem to decide whether to perch one
hip on the corner of his desk or retreat to the plush-
looking chair behind it.

It couldn't be that something had gone wrong with
Abir's recovery. Before she'd set off for the hospital that
morning she'd spoken to the anaesthetist who'd been
first on call last night, as well as the nurse who'd been
specialling him. Both had been very pleased with the
way his little body had coped with the trauma of such
major surgery, in spite of the fact that he was still very
heavily sedated.

And it had only been moments ago that she'd been
standing beside his high-tech cot, surrounded by the
clicks and bleeps of all the monitors, keen to reread his
notes and hold Meera Hanani's hand reassuringly, even
while she knew that nothing less than holding her baby
son in her arms, whole and healthy, was ever going to
be reassurance enough.

As for any problems with the other patients she'd
seen yesterday, she hadn't had time to get to the pile
of case notes so she had no idea what would have put
such a buttoned-down expression on his 'eminent consultant' face.

So, was it something she'd done…or failed to do?

For goodness' sake! Guessing just wasn't her way,
she thought impatiently.

'Is there a problem?' she demanded forthrightly, just

as the possibility that he was trying to find the words to give her the sack exploded into her brain.

'I am afraid… There is something…'

He made two false starts and she nearly growled with anxiety, suddenly realising just how much she did *not* want to lose this job.

It wasn't just that she needed to stay close to her grandmother, although that was essential to her plans for the foreseeable future. No, it was the blinding revelation that, much as she had been enjoying the work she'd been doing in Mr Breyley's unit, there was something so much *more* in what she'd seen and done yesterday.

And it wasn't just that her new boss was the most good-looking, sexiest…

Enough! she chided herself fiercely, knowing those sorts of thoughts were totally inappropriate, especially with her job on the line.

'I am sorry,' he said gruffly, and her worst fears were confirmed.

'Why?' she gulped, feeling too sick to be able to voice all the questions she wanted to ask.

Why did he want to sack her?

Why wasn't he willing to give her a second chance?

Why couldn't he…?

'I must apologise because I was unnecessarily rude and abrupt last night, and I completely forgot my manners. I totally forgot to thank you for your help.'

Emily was left floundering like a fish out of water, almost certain that her mouth was gaping like a fish's, too.

'You're *not* sacking me?' She hardly dared to believe it. She'd been so sure that…

'*Sacking* you? What on earth for?' he demanded,

but she noticed that he hadn't quite been able to bring himself to meet her eyes.

So he *had* considered it, she realised with a sudden heaviness inside her and a panicked feeling as if she'd only just realised how close her feet were to the edge of an unstable cliff.

Who would have thought that it would matter this much to her that she might never get to work with him again?

Still, he'd obviously changed his mind, the more optimistic side of her nature pointed out firmly. And that meant that she had more time to show him how good a doctor she could be, more time to make herself indispensable to him.

'You know as well as I do that you proved yourself more than competent in Theatre yesterday,' he continued, that deep, slightly husky voice sounding almost musical with the liquid syllables borrowed from his own tongue. And as for the unexpected praise...she could already feel a wash of heat sweeping up her throat and into her face.

'As for your help on the beach,' he continued, and it was his turn to sound almost embarrassed this time, 'I am not absolutely sure what you did, but I was able to walk all the way to the car park near the lifeboat station without having to stop, and the improvement seems to have held this morning, too. So I really do owe you my gratitude.'

'I'm glad you're feeling easier, and you're welcome,' she said, tempted to allow a broad grin to creep from ear to ear. Utter relief took the brakes off her tongue. 'So, are we going into Theatre again today? Will you be letting me assist again?'

'Have I created a monster?' he murmured, but she could see from the gleam in his eyes that he approved of her enthusiasm. 'We will be welcoming some new patients this afternoon. They flew into Heathrow airport from Xandar overnight and will be transferring by plane down to St Mawgan where they will be met by a translator and medical staff for the last part of the journey.'

'Let me guess who will be in charge of documenting their admission,' Emily grumbled, screwing her nose up at the sheer volume of paperwork that was always involved.

'You will also be in charge of leading the case conference session when all the different disciplines get their heads together,' he announced quietly, taking her breath away completely.

'This is a test isn't it?' she said nervously, guessing that at the very least there would probably be a top-flight surgeon from the plastics department as well as the anaesthetist at that meeting.

'Why not look at it as more of a challenge?' he suggested. 'You will have three patients with various problems and you will need to pull together their case histories, such as they are, and put together an up-to-date picture of their problems, their needs and at least one possible course of treatment.'

'Will that include blood work and X-rays?' She barely glanced up from the rapid notes she was taking, her heart already pumping at the task ahead.

'Of course. Everything we will need to make an informed decision about the best way to proceed. And in the meantime,' he added, 'do not forget to keep an eye on Abir. I am not expecting any problems, but Meera is delighted that you have been in to visit him. I am certain she appreciates the fact that you are a woman. Xandar is currently ruled by some very traditional men who continue to make it very difficult for women to feel comfortable in the company of men who are not their husbands or close family members.'

'She must be feeling very isolated over here,' Emily said, her heart going out to the young woman all over again. It must be so hard for her to be going through this while she was so far away from the support of her friends and family. 'That must make the whole situation even more fraught for her if she doesn't like to ask questions for fear of offending.'

'Exactly so,' he said quietly, 'and the language barrier just makes things even more difficult.'

'I shall have to learn some of your language,' Emily announced with a sudden flash of inspiration. 'Even if I can only manage a few words of greeting, it would be better than nothing. Would you teach me?'

He seemed almost as startled as she was to hear the request coming out of her mouth, but before she could hastily retract it, he was answering.

'Of course, if you are really interested in learning. But it is not one of the easiest languages,' he warned.

'So, you don't think I'll be fluent by the end of my time on the unit?' she teased as a bubble of excitement grew inside her. The idea of learning his language had been a spur-of-the-moment idea but the more she thought about it, the more she liked it, not least because it would mean she would have an excuse to spend more time in his company.

And how stupid was that? she berated herself once she was out of his presence. Ever since she'd first seen him on the beach there had been something about the man that had drawn her like a magnet. And now that she was working with him, the attraction seemed to be growing stronger so that all she could think about in his presence was the next time she would be with him. And as for her dreams last night, after the interlude on the darkening beach when she'd come to know the textures and warmth of his back as intimately as her own, well, they'd been enough to have her waking up that morning needing a cold shower to cool off.

'Dr Livingston, where is Mr Khalil? I must see him immediately,' announced an imperious voice that dragged her away from her vivid memories with a snap.

Of course it was Nasima Osman, his beautiful secretary, as immaculately dressed as ever and with such perfect hair and make-up that it must take her hours to get ready for work each day.

'He's just gone into the little conference room to talk with the parents of one of the patients, but he left strict instructions that he didn't want to be disturbed,' Emily told her with a glance towards the door, and was horrified when the arrogant young woman immediately headed towards it.

'Don't!' Emily cautioned sharply, but Nasima whirled on one slender heel to face her with an expression that reminded Emily of a spitting cat.

'His "do not disturb" only refers to *you*,' she announced haughtily. '*I* am *always* welcome,' and she turned back to open the forbidden door with a flourish.

'*Out! Now!*' Zayed snapped, his dark eyes angry as they met Emily's across the intervening yards. 'I told you I was *not* to be disturbed.'

'But, Zayed,' the young woman simpered. 'I have brought you a message that—'

'It can wait,' he growled, his impatience only too clear, as was the fact that he was blaming Emily for the interruption. 'Or give it to Emily. But shut that door *now*.'

The young woman pulled the door shut with a pout and a deliberately loud bang, then started to flounce her way out of the unit.

'What about the message?' Emily reminded her.

'I would not give any message to *you*,' Nasima snapped rudely. 'I will give it only to Zayed when he comes to me.'

'Suit yourself,' Emily murmured to the slender departing back, but she may as well have saved her breath. Anyway, the young woman's pettiness didn't matter when measured against the fact that she'd deliberately interrupted Zayed's meeting.

Emily knew just how important the conversation going on in that room was. Those poor parents were being faced with a terrible choice and the last thing they needed was to be disturbed.

Repeatedly she replayed the expression of annoyance on Zayed's face and wondered if she should have done more, if there had been any way she could have stopped his secretary from barging in like that.

'Zayed... Ah, Mr Khalil,' she corrected herself hurriedly when he finally emerged from the interview room, shocked to discover that she'd worked for Mr Breyley for almost a month without ever wondering whether she could call him by his first name, whereas, in her head, she was already calling this man Zayed after a single day.

'In a minute, please,' he said stiffly as he strode straight past her to his office and closed the door.

Her heart sank. He obviously thought it was her fault that he'd been interrupted, and if she were to say anything, it would look as if she was trying to shift the blame.

Still, it was important that she tried to set the record straight. She didn't want him to think that she would flagrantly flout a direct request, so she went to stand outside his door, determined to catch him before he was called elsewhere.

She could hear the low rumble of his voice behind the door and even though she wasn't deliberately listening to what he was saying, she quickly realised that there was no point even in trying. As his voice took on a louder, angrier note she could tell that he was speaking in his own language and she wouldn't have understood a word.

Suddenly the door was snatched open and his secretary emerged looking much less than her perfect self, with her heavy eye make-up smudged and her flawless olive-toned skin blotchy with a mixture of tears and temper.

'You!' she snarled when she saw Emily waiting there, then let loose with what was obviously a flood of invective.

'Enough! Go!' Zayed ordered icily, his expression looking as if had been carved from Cornish granite.

Emily's heart stuttered at the thought of having that much anger directed at her, but stood her ground. She knew she hadn't done anything wrong, but...

'Emily.' The edge to his voice made all her nerves jangle while she waited for the verdict but, instead of inviting her into his office to detail his displeasure, she actually saw the slightest lifting of his ire. 'There has been a mix-up in the arrangements, so the two of us will have to go to St Mawgan to meet the plane. We will need to leave in half an hour. In the meantime, would you contact the human resources department and ask them to find me a half-competent secretary? I have fired my previous one for misconduct…oh, and for being a totally useless secretary!'

Her head was whirling as he turned and disappeared into his office again, but she had no time to contemplate the recent turn of events.

Her hand hovered over the phone at the reception desk but she wasn't certain who to contact. She'd only been at St Piran's for a month so had no idea how to go about requesting staff.

'Problem?' asked Jenna Stanbury as she consulted the long printed list of numbers for the various hospital departments.

'I need to get in contact with Human Resources in a hurry,' Emily said, concentrating so hard on her search that she didn't consider how that would sound to someone else.

'Oh, Emily! You're not leaving us already!' Jenna exclaimed, seeming genuinely upset by the idea. 'What happened? Is it anything I can sort out for you?'

'No, it's not for me,' Emily reassured her, feeling quite heartened that her new colleague was disappointed at the thought of her departure. 'Zayed…Mr Khalil… asked me to find him a competent secretary.'

'A secretary?' Jenna's eyes grew round and a broad grin spread over her face. 'Whooee! You mean the fashion plate's been given the boot, without getting her hooks into him? Thank goodness for that. She's nowhere near good enough for him.'

'Not that you're biased or anything.' Emma chuckled, glad to know that she wasn't the only one who would be glad to see the back of the woman. 'Now, tell me how to find her replacement, quick, or she might have to stay.'

It was amazing how the mention of Zayed Khalil's name seemed to smooth everyone's feathers. All Emily had to do was say that he was the one needing a secretary in a hurry and the woman on the other end of the phone sounded as if she was falling over herself to find him someone competent.

'It's unlikely that I'll be able to find a bilingual one at such short notice,' she warned. 'Did he want to wait while I track one down or does he need someone straight away?'

'He definitely needs someone today,' Emily stressed, determined that there would be no possibility of a certain person having a chance to talk herself back into the job. 'The sooner the better, because we're expecting three new patients to fly into St Mawgan and we'll have to leave to collect them in under half an hour. If you've any idea of the amount of paperwork they'll be bringing with them—'

'Say no more,' the woman interrupted decisively. 'I'll do my best for him, even if I have to juggle some of the other secretarial staff around.'

'All sorted?' Jenna asked eagerly, when Emily had put the phone down.

'I hope so. She seemed to want to be helpful. Now all I've got to do is find out what I need to do to collect patients from the airport.'

'There should be preliminary files on them, if Madam hasn't made a complete mess of the system,' Jenna said with a grimace as she tried to access the information on the computer. 'Most of them are referred by their own physicians in Xandar, so there's a whole heap of stuff sent over to persuade Zayed to take them on.'

'Wouldn't it be better if they were treated in Xandar?' Emily asked. 'It would save them the stress and expense of having to travel thousands of miles to a strange country.'

'It would, if they had somewhere suitable to perform the operations and someone of Zayed's calibre willing to do the procedures,' Jenna said sombrely. 'Most of the ones who come over here are the children of the poorer people, the ones who live out in the more remote regions who wouldn't have the money to pay for the treatment even if they could get to it.'

'But...' That didn't make sense. 'If they're too poor to get the treatment in their own country, how can they possibly afford to come all the way to Cornwall?'

'They have a wealthy benefactor who pays for them,' Jenna said simply, then flicked a deliberate glance in the direction of Zayed's office door.

'Zayed?' Emily breathed, shocked to discover this whole new layer to the man's character.

'It's not generally known,' Jenna warned. 'He prefers that people just think he works here, not that he actually funds the unit personally.'

'Wow! A man with deep pockets.' She couldn't imagine how much such a set-up must cost.

'Very deep, hence his little gold-digger secretary.'

'That explains a lot, but it doesn't do anything towards getting ready to collect the new patients,' Emily pointed out.

'Well, just hang on a minute and I'll have some details printed out for you,' Jenna promised.

She was as good as her word, and by the time Zayed emerged from his office again, Emily had three neat files of basic information prepared and waiting.

'Ready?' he asked as he strode towards her, shrugging his shoulders to settle his suit jacket perfectly into position.

'Ready,' she agreed, reaching for the files even as her eyes greedily took in the way the width of his shoulders filled out the smooth pale fabric and the way the cut of the suit emphasised his lean waist and long legs.

There was no way her own summery skirt and top could compare with his elegance but, then, having heard what Jenna had told her about the man, there really was no comparison between the two of them on any level. He was obviously a very wealthy man while she was still paying off the debts she'd amassed during her training. He was sophisticated and had travelled widely while the furthest she'd ever gone had been to London. He was doubtless accustomed to lobster thermidor prepared in a Michelin-starred restaurant while she was far more familiar with fish and chips wrapped in paper and eaten on the beach in Penhally.

This was no time for a pity party for one, she reminded herself as she followed him, his long strides meaning that she almost had to jog to keep up with him. Anyway, what did it matter that the two of them had nothing in common? There was never any likelihood that there would be anything more than a professional relationship between them, no matter what her hormones wanted.

'You are thinking deep thoughts,' he commented as he bypassed the waiting ambulances and made for a sleek silver car.

'Aren't we going in the ambulance?' She hastily avoided the topic of her thoughts. There was no way she was going to tell him that she'd been thinking about the impossibility that he would ever be interested in her in a personal way.

'There are three ambulances,' he said with a gesture towards the three long-wheelbase estate cars that had been specially adapted for use as ambulances. 'Each one has a driver and a paramedic and there is room for the patient to be on a stretcher, in a wheelchair or sitting in an ordinary seat. There is also room for the parents to travel with their child, but there is no room for any extra bodies.'

'So, why do we need to go?' Emily asked as she made a mental note to find the time to take a closer look at those ambulances. From what she could see, as the three vehicles pulled out in convoy, each interior had been very carefully planned so that the paramedic would still be able to take proper care of his patient even while they were on the move. It would be interesting to find out how well they did the job and whether there were any drawbacks in comparison with the bigger box-on-wheels ambulances.

Zayed made an impatient sound as the three vehicles disappeared round the corner, not making any attempt to follow them, even though the engine of his car was already quietly purring. 'I will be there to act as translator and to provide any medical help that the paramedics are not qualified to administer.'

'So, what is my role?' she asked, wondering what he was waiting for.

'You are here to see how the organisation of these transfers is supposed to work, and to come up with any improvements that you can think of—and to provide protection.'

'Protection?' She blinked in surprise. 'From what?'

He nodded towards something he was watching over his shoulder and she glanced across to see the scowling figure of his ex-secretary making her way towards them with a large wheeled suitcase and a bulging shoulder-bag.

'We are giving Nasima a lift to the airport so that she can make the connection with a flight from Heathrow,' he said as he released his seat belt. 'She will be back in Xandar before midnight,' he added with what sounded suspiciously like relief, then got out of the car to stow her luggage.

Emily knew the exact second the young woman saw her sitting in the front of Zayed's car, and if looks could have shot poison, she would have been writhing in her death throes.

The journey took a little over half an hour and was one of the most uncomfortable journeys Emily had ever taken. Not because of the car or its driver, because both were excellent. No, it was the sullen black cloud sitting in the back seat that cast a pall over the journey, in spite of the fact that their route was taking them through some of the most beautiful Cornish countryside on a perfect golden September day.

At intervals, Nasima would mutter under her breath,

but obviously not quietly enough to disguise what she was saying if Zayed's stony face was any indication. Finally, he broke his silence, and Emily didn't need to understand a single word of the quietly spoken tirade to know that he was reading his former secretary the Riot Act.

It was a very chastened-looking woman who climbed out of the car at the airport and her tear-filled eyes as she gazed up at Zayed and her rapidly moving mouth told Emily that she was making an impassioned plea to be allowed to stay, but to no avail. Zayed silently unloaded her luggage onto a trolley, handed her a piece of paper that looked like an email flight confirmation and gestured towards the door.

The last Emily saw of Nasima Osman was the hate-filled glare sent her way before she turned and stalked into the building.

'I am sorry about that,' Zayed said as he settled himself back into the driving seat and started the engine. 'Her parents are friends of my family. They were concerned for her safety when she said she wanted to work abroad and when they heard I was setting up the unit in Penhally they asked me to…'

'Take her under your wing?' Emily suggested when he paused.

'Exactly,' he agreed. 'Except she was not happy to come somewhere so far away from the bright city lights and she seemed to think…'

He paused again and Emily was intrigued to see a wash of colour darken the high slash of his cheekbones. She almost chuckled aloud when she realised that he was embarrassed, but decided to spare his blushes.

'She decided that if she couldn't have the social life she wanted, you were going to be the consolation prize.'

Did he choke or was that a laugh, swiftly stifled?

'Something like that,' he admitted, but he seemed inordinately pleased that they'd reached the designated parking area for picking up incoming passengers. 'Do you want to stay with the car or...?'

'I won't learn very much about the way you organise things from here,' she pointed out as she released her seat belt and slid out of the sinfully comfortable leather seat. Once more she found herself trying to keep up with those long legs as he strode towards the plate-glass doors.

At the last moment he seemed to realise that she wasn't with him and paused to allow her to catch up.

'I am sorry,' he said with a rueful grin.

'It's all right for you people who can leap tall buildings at a single bound, but us mere mortals have to work a little harder at it,' she grumbled. 'I've always wished I was taller, then I wouldn't have to work so hard to keep the weight off because it wouldn't show so much.'

'You do not need to lose any weight!' he exclaimed. 'Your body is exactly right for...' He stopped abruptly, as though he'd only just realised what he was saying.

This time there was no mistaking the dark colour that flooded his face and Emily almost felt sorry for him. Almost, because she couldn't help being absurdly delighted that he'd said something so complimentary.

'I am sorry. It is not my place to make personal comments,' he said formally, and laughter bubbled out of her.

'Oh, *please*, don't apologise! That's the nicest thing anyone's ever said about me. When you're only five feet six and tend towards…shall we call it chubbiness…the compliments are rather few and far between.'

'Then the men you know are all idiots,' he growled. 'A real woman is not a handful of bones covered in skin. She has curves and softness so that when she holds her child…' He shut his mouth with a snap then muttered something under his breath before saying, 'I am sorry,' again and gesturing for her to precede him into the arrivals hall.

Emily knew that her smile must be stretching from ear to ear but she really didn't care—in fact, crazy as it sounded for someone of thirty years of age, her feet hardly felt as if they were touching the ground because Zayed had just said that a real woman should have curves and softness and he thought her body was exactly right.

CHAPTER FIVE

THE rest of that week soon disabused Emily of the idea that Zayed had any special interest in her.

He kept up a brutal pace.

She knew that he arrived at St Piran's in the early hours of the morning to deal with the unending office work entailed in the organisation of such a specialist unit, because he was always there before she arrived for her shift. He then continued through a twelve-hour shift of ward rounds, consultations, assessments and operations, and in between all that he still managed to find time to speak to worried parents and play with the children or just give them a comforting cuddle.

The only time she could be almost certain that he wouldn't be involved right up to his neck at the hospital was in the early evening, when the sun slid down over the western horizon. Then, unless there had been some sort of emergency on the ward or he'd been called down to consult in A and E, she knew she would probably be able to find him down on the wave-flattened sand on the beach in Penhally.

It was totally self-deluding, she knew, but that was when she'd come to think of him as *hers*, and of that time as their special time together, even though he never so much as glanced in her direction.

It had started the very evening after his back had seized up on him.

As usual, she'd been to visit Beabea, but as her disease was progressing, she was alert for less and less time as the morphine kicked in. Rather than sit there staring at the visible signs that her beloved grandmother was fading away in front of her eyes, Emily had taken to running from the hospice unit down to the beach.

She was honest enough to admit to herself that it wasn't just displacement activity so that she could switch off from what was happening up in that almost silent room. It had rapidly become an essential part of her day to see that tall, tanned figure stride down onto the sand and strip off to begin his self-imposed routine.

Today was no different.

She'd actually caught herself clock-watching when it had looked as if she might have to stay late, and her concern wasn't just that she might not arrive until Beabea was already asleep. But here she was, once more sitting in the shadows among the rocks, with her pulse tripping with crazy excitement at the prospect of seeing the man she'd been working with all day.

'So, this is where you hide,' said a familiar voice, and she almost leapt out of her skin.

'Zayed!' she squeaked when he loomed over her, silhouetted against a spectacular peach and lavender sunset, then coloured even more furiously when she realised that once again she'd actually used his given name to his face.

'I saw you looking at your watch earlier today, just after you had been holding Abir, and then you disappeared,' he complained. 'I was not certain whether you were on late duty this evening or whether you would be here as my guardian.'

Emily suddenly realised that she'd never explained the special dispensation she'd been granted by Mr Breyley and felt a sharp pang of concern that her current freedom from on-call duties might not continue.

'I'm sorry, Mr Khalil, I should have told you about that,' she started to babble, her brain totally scrambled by the possibility that she might not be able to visit Beabea for days if the arrangement were rescinded. 'Mr Breyley arranged that I should be allowed to live so far away from St Piran's so that I would be able to visit my grandmother. That's why I'm not on the on-call roster at the moment, but when…as soon as…'

'Hush, hush! Calm yourself,' he soothed in exactly the same way that he calmed their little patients when everything became too much for them. 'There was obviously some good reason why the arrangement was made this way, and I have no complaints about the work you do when you are on duty. Now…' His tone of voice changed completely. 'Are you just going to watch me or are you going to do some exercise, too?'

Emily's emotions were in complete turmoil.

She didn't think she would ever be able to talk about her grandmother's illness and her inevitable loss without choking up, but at the same time the fact that this handsome, charismatic man seemed to be inviting her to keep him company this evening was enough to double her pulse rate in seconds.

'Have you already been running?' he asked, as if she weren't standing there with her mouth hanging open

and her eyes glued to the expanse of taut male flesh he
was uncovering right in front of her.

'Uh, n-not yet,' she managed to stammer, finally
managing to drag her covetous gaze away. She could
remember all too clearly just what that skin and those
muscles felt like and her fingertips were tingling with
the desire to touch them again.

'Well, then, if you go for your run now, you could
join me when I am ready for my swim,' he suggested.
'You do swim, do you not?'

Emily rolled her eyes. 'Beabea never allowed me
down to the beach by myself until I could prove that I
could swim well enough. Then I completed a lifesaving
course so I could be useful if anyone else got into difficulties. The lifeguards can't be on duty twenty-four
hours a day.'

'And that is why you insisted on watching over me
when I was breaking all the rules,' he said with a nod of
comprehension, but Emily wasn't going to tell him that
it wasn't only the fact that he'd gone in to swim on his
own that had prompted her to wait for him to emerge
that first evening. There was no way she would be ad-
mitting that it had also been the prospect of catching
another glimpse of that beautifully sculpted body.

Emily had set off for her first trip to the end of the
beach when she wondered whether it would be a good
idea to go swimming with Zayed after all.

Although he'd seemed perfectly friendly so far
this evening, she had definitely been aware that he'd
created a deliberate distance between the two of them
after their last encounter.

Had he resented her presence here? After all,
Penhally was a rather long way to go if he only wanted

to find a beach to do his exercises and finish up with a swim. It might be that he'd deliberately come this far so that there was less likelihood of bumping into anyone who would recognise him.

There was also the isolation factor.

This late in the season there were far fewer holidaymakers about, especially the school or university students who might linger on the beach that much later in the day. This would almost guarantee that he wouldn't have an audience while he pushed himself to the limit to regain his strength and flexibility.

He certainly wasn't struggling so much this evening, she noticed as she passed him for the third time, only now allowing herself to notice that, as she was sticking to the very edge of the firm sand, she was between him and the dying sun and was therefore not limited to seeing him as a silhouette. In fact, this was the clearest view she'd ever had of him, apart from the glimpse of firm male flesh she was treated to when he leaned forward in his V-necked scrubs.

Just then he turned to pick up his towel and as she got her first good look at the injury that had made his struggles so necessary, she almost tripped over her own feet.

Dear Lord, what *had* happened to him?

She'd felt the irregularity of his skin when she'd been working out the knots in his muscles—she hadn't been able to avoid feeling it—but in the poor light she'd never realised just how livid the scarring had been, or how extensive.

'It was an explosion,' he said suddenly, and she was horrified to realise that she'd been standing there staring at his injuries.

'That would explain the type of scarring,' she said, finally managing to grab hold of a little of the control she'd learned during her training. 'Did you need a great deal of surgery and skin grafts?'

'Not as much as I might have done if the spinal cord had been severed,' he said prosaically, and the image of such a vital man being confined to a wheelchair made her shudder.

She wanted to know more. In fact, she wanted to know everything there was to know about this man, but before she could formulate the next question he was gesturing towards the sea.

'Ready to swim?' he invited.

She actually put both hands to the hem of her top, ready to strip it off over her head, before she remembered the reason why she couldn't.

'I'm not wearing a costume under my clothes,' she said with a grimace, and the feeling of disappointment was immediate. If she'd thought about it earlier, she could have run back to Beabea's cottage to change. It had been so long since she'd swum with anyone, and the thought of sharing this stretch of the sea with him was...

'You are wearing sports clothes under those things, are you not?' he asked, gesturing towards the casual clothing she'd donned before she'd left the hospital. 'Can you not swim in those?'

'Why not?' she exclaimed with a grin when she suddenly remembered that her sports bra and pants were the sort of utilitarian shape that wouldn't look unlike a modest bikini.

Before she could second-guess herself and realise that she was exposing far more than she ought to the man,

she stripped her cotton knit top over her head and shoved
the drawstring trousers over her hips to pool around her
ankles.

With the sort of burning awareness that told her he
was watching her every step, she sprinted for the water.
Barely waiting for the waves to reach above her knees,
she dived through the next line of surf and came up
with her arm already poised for the first fierce stroke.

It was some time before she realised that Zayed had
stopped swimming and was now standing in the fading light on the beach.

This time he'd been the one standing guard while
she'd ploughed backwards and forwards across the
mouth of the bay until her muscles began to quiver in
a way that told her she'd regret this in the morning.

'I hadn't realised just how much I'd missed that. Have
you been waiting a long time?' she asked, panting as she
splashed her way through the shallows towards him. It
was only when he didn't reply that she looked a little
more closely and realised that he seemed to be trans-
fixed by her appearance…her almost naked appearance as the waning light rendered her coffee-coloured
clothing all but invisible against her tanned skin, and
the cool sea breeze puckered her nipples into tight little
beads.

'Here,' he said gruffly, holding out his own towel
in her direction, then dragged his gaze away to stare
fixedly towards the fading horizon.

Emily's breath caught in her throat as she stepped
close enough to take the nubby fabric from him to wrap
it around her shoulders, wishing she was able to see his
expression more clearly.

For just a second it had seemed as if there had been

something almost…almost predatory in those dark eyes
as they'd skimmed over her, and the thought that he'd
been looking at her with sexual intent sent an atavis-
tic thrill right through her that was waking all sorts of
primitive responses.

'Why do you…?'

'What is it…?'

They both hurried into speech to fill the uncomfortable silence stretching between them, and both halted
at the same time.

'What did you want to know?' he offered as he pulled
the edges of his shirt together and began to button away
the sight of that impressive chest.

'Oh, I just wondered…' What *had* she been thinking about while her body had still been reacting to the
thought that he might have liked what he'd seen? Oh,
yes. 'Why do you come all the way to Penhally to swim?
Is it because it's far enough from St Piran's so that
you're unlikely to bump into someone who'd recognise
you?'

'If that was the reason, it obviously did not work,' he
said wryly. 'But, actually, it is because it is convenient
for me as I have a house up there.' He gestured towards
the far end of the beach, to the cliffs beyond Penhally
Bay.

Emily knew the area he meant and knew the sort of
houses that had been built up there.

'The view must be spectacular,' she said, even as
she silently acknowledged that only someone wealthy
enough to set up a specialist unit would be able to afford
one of those houses. They were a far cry from Beabea's
little cottage.

'And what is it that has you hurrying to Penhally

every day?' he asked as he accepted the neatly folded towel from her and tucked it under one arm. 'I saw you looking at your watch today, just after it was time for you to leave. Do you have a man waiting impatiently for you to come—?'

The shrill sound of a mobile phone cut through his unexpectedly personal question and Emily reached for it, recognising the ring tone. She caught sight of the name of the person ringing her and her heart suddenly leapt into her mouth.

'Hello?' she said, breathless with dread.

'Hello, Emily, love.' Her grandmother's gentle voice filled her ear with the reassurance that she hadn't gone yet. 'Staff Nurse let me use her phone to tell you that I'm awake if you want to visit. I didn't know if you might have given up on me and gone back—'

'Of course I want to see you,' Emily cut in. 'I've just been for a swim on the beach down below you, but it won't take long for me to get there. Five minutes. Ten at the most.'

She ended the call and turned to the silent shadow standing beside her with a smile. 'That's the reason why I hurry to Penhally every day.'

'Your boyfriend expects you to stop what you are doing to come when he calls?' he asked, and in the darkness his voice sounded almost disapproving.

'No.' She chuckled. 'That wasn't a demanding boyfriend. That was my grandmother.' She was struck by the sudden urge to introduce the two of them to each other. It would be interesting to see what Beabea made of the man who'd begun to fill her every waking thought. 'Would you like to walk up with me to visit her? She had to move into the hospice a few days ago and...'

'The hospice? She is ill?' She was almost certain he'd intended refusing the invitation until that moment.

'She has inoperable cancer,' Emily told him, the words no easier to say than the first time she'd ever said them. 'She's unlikely to live until October.'

'Surely she will not want a stranger to intrude upon her?' They were walking while they were talking and she could see his expression a little better now that they were climbing closer to the lights along Harbour Road, well enough to see that he was intrigued.

'Beabea has never met a stranger,' she said with a chuckle. 'It has never mattered to her whether someone is a duke or a dustman—she is just fascinated by people and always finds a way to put them at their ease.'

'Even now, when she is—?'

'Especially now,' Emily broke in, preventing him from saying the hateful words. 'She has been complaining that she hasn't had enough visitors to make life interesting. I think she would definitely find *you* interesting.'

He laughed aloud, the sound bouncing merrily back at them from the row of houses that faced out towards the sea. 'In that case, how can I refuse the invitation?'

'Beabea? Are you still awake?' Emily called gently as she stuck her head round the door.

'Come in, Emily, dear,' her grandmother invited. 'I'm sorry I was asleep when you came earlier. They had to change the dose on that dratted pump thing. I have no intention of sleeping my last few days away if I can help it.'

'Are you feeling up to a visitor?' Emily asked, every nerve aware of Zayed's presence in the corridor behind her as she stepped forward to give her grandmother a gentle hug.

'Of course I am, dear.' Her faded blue eyes brightened at the prospect, even though she was now barely strong enough to lift her hand in an automatic gesture to check that her soft silvery curls were tidy. 'I hope you've brought someone entertaining.'

'I do not know how entertaining I will be, but it is an honour to meet the grandmother of Emily,' Zayed said as he stepped into the room and walked forward to offer his hand. 'I am Zayed Khalil and I work with your granddaughter at St Piran's Hospital.' He bent low over Beabea's hand and Emily saw delight sparkle in her eyes even as she took his measure.

'Emily has spoken of you,' she said after several long seconds of the sort of silence that would have had Emily shuffling her feet when she'd been younger. Zayed stoically stood his ground and seemed to have no difficulty meeting her grandmother's direct gaze until she gave a single nod and a smile.

'I am very pleased to meet you,' she said, and Emily could hardly blame her for sounding almost coquettish in the face of Zayed at his most charming. 'But she completely forgot to tell me how handsome you are,' Beabea added, and Emily cringed.

'Perhaps Emily does not think I am handsome,' Zayed retorted with a sideways glance and an unrepentant grin at Emily's blazing face

Her grandmother snorted. 'I didn't bring up a stupid grandchild,' Beabea told him sternly. 'She knows a good man when she sees one.'

It was something that she'd heard her grandmother say a thousand times over the years, but it was the first time Emily had ever seen it bring such a look of sadness to a man's face. And she had absolutely no idea why. Zayed *was* a handsome man and he was also a good man, otherwise he would never have thought about setting up the unit at St Piran's and working the hours he did to take care of his little charges.

And as for the way he was gently teasing her grandmother, bringing a touch of colour to cheeks that had been grey and lifeless for so many weeks…well, if that wasn't a mark of a good-natured man, Emily didn't know what was.

Within moments, Zayed had been invited to perch on the edge of Beabea's bed and was being given the third degree. All Emily had to do was stay in the background, listening quietly to learn that he'd been born and brought up in Xandar and had returned there after he'd completed his medical training, only leaving in the wake of the most recent wave of atrocities.

'I remember,' her grandmother said thoughtfully. 'There was a series of explosions, wasn't there? Several prominent people were killed when one of the more reactionary groups tried to make a point.'

'There is nothing wrong with your memory,' Zayed said, and Emily was sure that some odd sort of understanding seemed to pass between the two of them, but then Beabea was back in full flow again.

'So, where are you living now?' she demanded. 'In one of those dreadful little flats they put up for the single staff who have to live close enough to reach the hospital when they're on call?'

'Thankfully, no,' he said with a grimace. 'Because

my unit is largely privately funded, I have been able to set many of the rules myself, including employing enough staff so that the on-call times are not too onerous. This means that I am able to live in my house in Penhally most of the time and travel backwards and forwards to the hospital.'

'You have a house in Penhally?' Beabea's tone was one of disgust that she'd missed out on this prime piece of gossip. 'Where? Do you know the name of the person who lived there before you?'

Emily suddenly blessed the inspiration that had prompted her to bring Zayed to visit her grandmother. In just these few short minutes she was hearing the answer to all the questions she'd been wanting to ask but hadn't dared to for fear of seeming too inquisitive.

'The house is up on the cliffs on the other side of Penhally, looking out across the water, like your room here. And as for the person who lived there before, he was one of the doctors who worked at the surgery down in the town. An Italian, I think, by the name of Marcus...'

'Marco,' her grandmother corrected him swiftly. 'Marco Avanti. He and his wife have gone back to Italy. But...if you're living in Marco's house, that means that you're the person who's set up that special unit for the children.'

'I told you all about the unit, Beabea,' Emily cut in, wondering if this confusion was a sign that it was time for the two of them to leave her in peace. If the morphine pump had recently delivered her next dose of analgesia, it wouldn't be long before she fell asleep again. 'Do you remember? Mr Khalil was kind enough to take me onto his team when Mr Breyley had to fly out to New Zealand.'

'Ah, yes! I meant to ask you about that. How is that little grandchild of his doing?' Beabea was momentarily distracted. 'How soon after the baby was born were they going to have to operate?'

'He phoned St Piran's to tell us that the operation has already been done,' Emily told her with a smile. 'They've detached all the faulty plumbing around the heart and put it all back where it should have been in the first place, and everything's looking good now.'

'Thank goodness for that,' her grandmother said with a nod of satisfaction. 'But I still want to know about this rehabilitation place of yours, young man. The gossip says that there are dozens of children up there, living a life of luxury with gold taps and marble floors and people to wait on them hand, foot and finger.'

'And I'm sure your language has just as many sayings about those who listen to gossip as mine does,' he said with a laugh.

'So, what *is* the truth, then?' Beabea pressed him.

'The truth is that it *was* a very luxurious house,' he admitted, 'but it was the position and the space and the possibility of converting it to my requirements that made me buy it. I knew I was going to need somewhere suitable for my little patients to go when they were well enough to leave St Piran's but not yet well enough to travel back to Xandar, and it had the added benefit of a wide view of the sea and proximity to the beach, which is something none of these children have ever seen or experienced before.'

'And the life of luxury with gold taps and servants?'

'A figment of the imagination, I am sorry to say. The

servants are really nursing and physiotherapy staff, and they are there to take care of the children and to show their parents how to continue the work when they return home.' He threw a quizzical glance in Emily's direction. 'Perhaps Emily could bring you over for a visit, so that you can tell all your friends about the real story.'

'I would love to,' Beabea said, but smiled a little sadly. 'Unfortunately, I think my visiting days are over, and I wouldn't like to upset your little patients if they saw such a sick old lady. But that doesn't mean that Emily can't come in my place,' she suggested, just a shade too brightly for Emily's liking. 'Then she could tell me all about it instead.'

'Beabea,' Emily began, embarrassed that Zayed might feel that he'd been forced into inviting her.

'I would be delighted to show Emily around,' he interrupted swiftly. 'In fact, I will be going on there this evening, when you have had enough of our company. Perhaps she will want to go with me then?'

CHAPTER SIX

As EMILY led the way out to her car a few minutes later, Zayed was still marvelling at the elderly woman's strength and determination, even though her body was failing her.

In those first few seconds when he'd stepped into the room it had felt very much like the times when he'd been called to stand under the eagle eye of his own grandmother, and he'd felt the same crazy conviction that she could read his mind and the same boyish need to fidget.

Then she'd silently nodded and smiled at him, and it had almost felt like some sort of blessing.

He was glad that he hadn't been tempted to underestimate the woman's intelligence, especially when the conversation had turned to his home country. Who would have thought that an elderly woman dying of cancer in the depths of Cornwall would have such accurate recall of the potentially catastrophic happenings in Xandar, a country so many thousands of miles away? And who would have believed that she would have so accurately connected those events with his own life?

He was only grateful that she hadn't questioned him about those dark times in front of Emily. It was some sort of relief to be working with someone who didn't know all the details and wouldn't be tempted to pity him for all he'd lost. Pity was one emotion that he couldn't bear, not when he didn't deserve it.

If it hadn't been for him…

'If you'd rather I didn't go to your house, just say so,' Emily said suddenly. 'Beabea did rather Shanghai you into making the invitation.'

By that time they had made their way around the curve of Penhally harbour wall and the row of shops, cafés and hotels that faced the tightly enclosed bay. They were approaching the turning for the car park by the life-boat station by the time she finally broke the silence in her little car.

'Do you not want to see where the children go when they leave the hospital?' He was suddenly disappointed that she might not want the guided tour he'd been look-ing forward to. There was something about her sheer enthusiasm for everything she did that seemed to lift the spirits of everyone around her, and he certainly wasn't immune.

'Of course I want to see it!' she exclaimed impa-tiently, and he had to suppress a satisfied smile at the thought that he was coming to know her so well. 'Apart from anything else,' she continued as she pulled neatly to the kerb, 'Beabea would never forgive me if I didn't come back to her with all the details.'

'Why do you call her Beabea?' He'd been curious ever since he'd heard the name. 'Is it the Cornish word for grandmother?'

'No.' She chuckled, a delightful sound that wrapped intimately around him in the semi-darkness of her car.

'If I remember rightly, grandmother is *henvamm* or *henvammow*.'

'So, why Beabea?' he persisted.

'Because her name is Beatrice,' Emily said simply, then decided to give him the full explanation. 'At the time I came to live with her, she had two friends… twins…who always did everything together, but one was always half a beat behind the other. So when they called her Bea, it sounded as if they were saying Beabea. I imitated them and it just stuck.'

'Do they still call her Beabea?'

'No.' She sighed. 'They're both gone now; so many of her lifelong friends have gone. That's one of the reasons why she's so delighted when I bring her visitors.'

Zayed thought about his own family—the remnants of it, at least—and suddenly realised just how long it had been since he'd seen them. His grandfather and the collection of great-aunts had all been well when he'd last seen them, but who knew what toll the years had taken? Any one of them could be in the same situation as Emily's grandmother.

Not that he could do anything about it. He was the very last person they would want to see on their doorstep.

'So, do you want me to drive you up to the house, or shall I follow you?' Emily asked, and he realised with a start of surprise that he must have been sitting lost in his thoughts for several minutes.

'You could follow me up there,' he suggested, releasing his seat belt and unfolding himself from the cramped position, grateful to find that his back hadn't seized up in the time since he'd climbed into her little car. 'Then you will have transportation to escape when you are too bored.'

'I'm still not certain I should be going *anywhere* when I look such a mess,' she complained with a despairing flick at the damp tangled ends of her hair. 'I haven't even got a comb with me and it looks like a rat's nest…a *salty* rat's nest. I should have stopped off at the cottage on the way past and done something about it.'

'You will not find any of the patients complaining,' he promised as he ducked back down to look at her, lit only by the courtesy light inside the car. 'Most of them will probably think you are some kind of exotic sea creature with your long wavy hair and your green eyes.'

He wasn't immune either. She looked perfectly stunning without a scrap of cosmetics on her skin, fresh and youthful and…and everything he had no right to be looking at.

'If you're sure?' she said doubtfully.

'I *am* sure.' He closed the car door to stride across the car park to his own vehicle.

It only took a few minutes to turn up past the surgery and climb the hill onto the top of the cliffs, and from there it was a relatively short run to the driveway leading to the strikingly modern house with the commanding view over both town and sea.

The security lights came on as soon as they approached the house and he signalled for Emily to draw up beside him, close to the front entrance.

'A word of warning,' he said as he reached for the door, suddenly unaccountably nervous about taking her inside. For some crazy reason, it really mattered what this young woman thought of the facility he was setting up here. 'Because they have a sleep in the middle of the day, not all of the children will be in bed yet, and it can be a little noisy.'

'A *little* noisy?' Emily echoed a few minutes later when she could almost hear herself think, again.

When Zayed had opened the door there had been a couple of seconds of absolute silence as everyone had looked to see who had arrived, and then the place had erupted into chaos, with every child shrieking for attention at the same time, each one with a smile from ear to ear as soon as they saw him.

Emily realised that she may just as well have been invisible as far as his little charges were concerned, and she slipped in quietly and closed the door, quite content to stand to one side and watch what was happening.

Those who were mobile had mobbed him and he'd rapidly disappeared under a maul of bodies, arms and legs, many sporting casts of varying lengths and colours. Those unable to join in had been forced to shout for attention in what was obviously a regular occurrence, while a scattering of their carers and parents looked on indulgently.

For a moment Emily had been worried that the children might be in danger of re-injuring themselves until she saw just how gently Zayed was treating them in spite of his blood-curdling growls.

'He should have children of his own…lots of children,' said a middle-aged woman who was obviously from Xandar, too, her accent full of the same liquid syllables as her countrymen that Emily had met on the unit at St Piran's. 'Taking care of other people's children is good but it will never fill the empty space inside him.'

Emily had an instant vision of dark-haired children with cheeky grins and the same gold-shot dark eyes that she saw over Zayed's mask every day, then ruthlessly shut the images away, refusing to let herself think about his eventual children. There was so little likelihood that they would be her children, too, that the thought of him surrounded by them was sharp enough to cause a physical pain around her heart.

'I am Reza Saleh,' the woman introduced herself, and settled herself comfortably against the wall beside Emily. 'I was one of those who worked with Zayed in our own country, before tragedy struck. Then, when I heard he needed staff over here in Penhally...' She shrugged eloquently. 'I learned English so I can come here to help him.'

'Reza! Come and save me from these terrible children!' Zayed called, then used exactly the same inflection when he said something in his own language, so it wasn't just the children's hilarity that told her he'd said the same thing again.

'Time for bed, children,' Reza said firmly with a clap of her hands, and copied Zayed in translating the order to their little charges.

'Not bed! No!' called several voices, obviously not tired of their game yet.

'No bed, no story,' Reza decreed in no-nonsense tones, and the children clearly understood that threat without the need for any translation.

Zayed was still helping the last of the children to their feet when someone caught sight of Emily for the first time.

Within seconds they were all staring at her as though she were an alien from another planet, their sudden silence erupting into a welter of incomprehensible questions.

'OK! OK!' Zayed called, putting both hands up in the air to call for silence as he made his way across to her. To her surprise he took her hand in his to lead her forward into their midst, then apparently forgot to let go because she ended up standing there surrounded by inquisitive children and adults with the warm strength of his hand wrapped around hers.

'This is Emily Livingston,' he said slowly and clearly, while she tried to work out exactly why it felt so right to stand there like that. 'She is a doctor at the hospital. She helps me to fix bones.' He repeated the simple sentences in their language to make sure they had all understood, but one little girl began shaking her head.

'No! No dotor!' she insisted, wide-eyed, then reverted to her own tongue for several impassioned sentences.

Several of the adults chuckled, including Zayed.

'What did she say?' Emily demanded softly.

'That you are too beautiful to be a doctor,' he said with a definite twinkle in his dark eyes. 'That you are really a princess who will wave your magic over them to make them well.'

'If only it were that easy,' Emily murmured, even as her pulse responded to his expression. 'Hello,' she said to the little girl, finally forcing herself to break the connection between their hands so that she could crouch down to bring them to more or less the same height. 'My name is Emily. What is your name?'

This time it was Reza who translated for her, and supplied the dark-haired moppet's name in return.

'This is Leela, and I don't think she'll ever believe

you're not a princess,' she said with a grin. 'Just look around the room and see if there are any other people here with blonde hair and green eyes.'

Blonde hair full of dried seawater so that it was as stiff as baler twine and green eyes with the most attractive dark shadows under them, either from too many hours spent worrying about Beabea or from too many nights spent dreaming about a certain dark-eyed consultant, to say nothing about coping with a demanding job.

Most attractive, she thought wryly, except that to one little girl, it was obviously good enough.

Reza clapped her hands again. 'Bed or no story,' she reminded her little charges, but little Leela wasn't going to be hurried, planting herself right in front of Emily to pose an urgent question.

'Leela has decided that she wants *you* to tell them the story tonight,' Zayed informed her with a grin as he gently lifted the little girl up to his shoulder.

Emily was barely aware that her feet were automatically taking her in his wake. 'Me? I can't tell them a story. I don't know any stories.'

'Oh, I am sure you will think of something,' he said airily as he led the way into what looked like an extremely well-appointed paediatric ward, albeit one that would have the most fantastic panoramic views once the sun came up in the morning.

'This is amazing,' Emily breathed as she looked around. There was everything any of the children might need to make life easier while they were hampered by casts and frames, but the decoration of the room and the colourful bedding and piles of toys gave it a very different feeling. And with the combination of the high staff-

ing level and parents eager to do anything they could
to help, it wasn't long before everyone was in pyjamas
and nightdresses and smelling of toothpaste.

'Story,' Leela said eagerly, as she held up a slim book
for Emily to see.

'"*The Little Mermaid*",' she read on the cover, and
when she heard Zayed choking back laughter she knew
where that suggestion had come from. 'Oh, I'm sure we
can think of something else.'

'You do not want to tell the story of the little mermaid who falls in love with the handsome prince?'

Emily had an uncomfortable feeling that it wouldn't
just be a story in a book if she didn't get herself under
better control. Seeing him by Abir's cot that first morning had definitely had an unexpected effect on her heart,
but learning about this other side to the man had pushed
her dangerously close to falling in love with him.

For all the good it would do her, she admitted wryly.
He was definitely every inch the elegant gentleman
good enough to be a prince, but she was a long way
from being the mermaid he would fall in love with.

Anyway, that sort of thing only happened in fairy-
tales.

Looking at the books on the bookshelf, her eyes fell
on several old favourites from her own childhood and
she exclaimed with delight before pausing for a moment,
wondering how on earth she was going to tell any story
when she couldn't speak a word of the children's language.

'There is a problem?' Zayed asked when she scanned
the titles, some in English and some in Arabic, and her
shoulders slumped when she realised that the task would
be all but impossible.

'There are so many wonderful stories, but I have no way of telling any of them,' she mourned.

'So simplify the story and tell it to me, and I will translate it for them,' Zayed suggested. 'Come. Sit here and begin.'

Emily hesitated when he beckoned her towards the seat beside him, knowing she ought to be sensible, but the temptation to be that close to him was suddenly too great to resist.

'Leela is very insistent that you read this one,' Reza said with a twinkle in her eye as she handed Emily the copy of *The Little Mermaid*.

The picture on the cover was the traditional one with the fish's tail replacing the young woman's legs, but Emily was sure she'd never noticed before that she was shown with long blonde hair curling over her shoulders to disguise the fact that she wasn't wearing a bikini, or that she was quite so well endowed.

'You also swim like a mermaid,' said a husky voice in her ear, and Emily turned shocked eyes towards a face that was suddenly as full of mischief as one of their young audience.

Was he implying that she had looked like the illustration, too, down on the beach this evening?

And if ever there was an inappropriate thought to have when surrounded by a dozen sharp-eyed strangers…

'Once upon a time…' Emily began, firmly refusing to acknowledge Zayed's presence beside her in anything other than his current role as translator.

Several pages in, she had the sneaking suspicion that his translations bore little relationship to what she was reading, especially when most of them were greeted with gales of laughter.

Leela seemed to be the only one who didn't appreciate his version and there was a decidedly militant look on her little face when she finally closed the book that told Emily that the story definitely hadn't ended the way she wanted it to.

'No! No!' she insisted even as the rest of their audience was applauding.

The sparkle of tears in those big dark eyes was more than Emily could stand.

'What is she saying?' she demanded, turning to face Zayed when Leela voiced her vehement disapproval. 'Why is she so upset?'

Zayed had the grace to look a little sheepish. 'She is not happy that I…took a few liberties with the story.'

'So, what does she want? Shall I start reading again?' Emily offered.

'It is not so much the story that is the problem,' he admitted. 'It is the ending.'

'I don't understand. What ending? There is only one ending.'

There was a hint of colour tingeing his cheeks as the little girl stood right in front of him, obviously telling him in great detail where he'd gone wrong.

'She says that the prince has to fall in love with the mermaid and give her a kiss so they can live happily ever after.'

'And that wasn't the way you translated it.' Emily could all too easily understand the reason for all the laughter before. She fixed him with a stern gaze, then suggested sweetly, 'So, tell the story that way, Mr

Consultant. It's not worth upsetting her just before she goes to bed.'

If anything, his embarrassment deepened and Emily suddenly became aware that the two of them were the focus of some hilarity from their adult audience, too, and not a little horrified fascination.

'I *have* tried to tell her, but she has convinced herself that you are the mermaid princess and that I should...'

Emily stared at him when the full import of what he *wasn't* saying poured over her.

Suddenly she was very aware of the fact that their bodies were touching from shoulder to knee and could almost swear that she could feel the temperature rising around them. Any hotter, and the settee would burst into flames.

She couldn't drag her eyes away from his, totally aware of everything from the sinful dark length of each individual eyelash to the way his pupils were dilating in evidence of his own awareness.

This was crazy. There was absolutely nothing between the two of them other than their professional relationship, but as the seconds stretched out it felt like something else entirely, and she didn't know whether to laugh or run away and hide.

What she did know was that all of a sudden she couldn't wait to see what Zayed was going to do. Was he going to find some other way of calming Leela down, or was he actually going to lean over and press his lips to hers...an act that she was almost certain would be forbidden in his own country.

One dark eyebrow rose, almost as if he'd read her thoughts, and a wicked smile teased the corner of his mouth as he reached for her hand.

'Oh, beautiful mermaid princess,' he intoned, then turned to Leela, obviously providing the enthralled youngster with her own personal translation, as though the rest of the room wasn't waiting breathlessly to see what would unfold.

'I am the handsome prince and I have found you at last,' he continued, staring soulfully into her eyes with enough simulated heat to set her tangled, salty hair on fire before switching the expression off to break into translation mode.

'Tell me you will give me your hand and we will live happily ever after,' he finished with a dramatic flourish, bringing her hand up to his lips to press a kiss to the backs of her fingers.

Emily barely heard his voice as he translated his final declaration. All she was aware of was the lingering heat and unexpected softness of his mouth where it had touched her.

'It is *your* turn,' he muttered out of the corner of his mouth, his eyes sparkling with glee, almost as if he knew how badly he'd scrambled her nerves.

'Oh, handsome prince, of course you can have my hand,' she said with a simpering smile and fluttering eyelashes, only to add under her breath, 'As long as you remember to give it back before I need it to drive home.'

It felt good to see him fighting laughter as he announced to the room, 'She said yes!' in both languages, and to be a part of the happy cheers that greeted the announcement.

And it wasn't just the memory of Leela's satisfied little face that had her feeling good when it was time to take her leave. This time she'd spent with Zayed had convinced her that underneath the driven professional persona he showed to the rest of the world, there was a gentle, generous man who would make a wonderful husband and father.

'Are you sure you don't want a cup of coffee before you leave?' he offered, as he stood with her by the front door.

The house behind them was largely silent now, with all the children safely tucked up in their beds even if they weren't all asleep yet. Most of the staff and parents had either gathered in the kitchen for a restorative cup of tea or coffee or had retired to their rooms, too, knowing that the morning would bring another exhausting, activity-filled day.

'I'd better not,' she said, even as a large part of her was aching to spend even a little more time with him. 'I wouldn't want to be late for work in the morning or my boss wouldn't be very happy.'

'He is a slave driver?' Zayed asked, and the smile in his voice told her he'd quickly understood that she was teasing him.

'Actually, no, he isn't,' she said honestly, keen to give credit where it was due. 'He's an excellent boss and works harder than anyone on his team.'

Emily caught her breath and bit her tongue sharply, suddenly conscious of the extra warmth that had infused the words. She'd only recently become aware of the feelings that had been growing since the first time she'd seen him. Had she betrayed too much?

'Well, now that he knows about your home situation, you can be sure that he will not have a problem if you should have to leave suddenly to be with your grandmother.'

If there was anything he could have said that would have been more calculated to bring tears to her eyes, Emily didn't know what it was.

'Thank you for that,' she said, and had to blink hard. 'But the oncologist was fairly certain of the course that her illness would take and how long…' Her throat closed up, filled with the huge lump of misery that was never far away.

'Ah, Emily, you know as well as I do that with any disease process there are no certainties,' he reminded her, and reached for her hand just as he had when they had been sitting side by side not long ago. 'Just know that I will understand if you need extra time to be with her. She is a lovely lady.'

'Thank you,' she managed to whisper, and had to force herself to retrieve her hand from his warm strength and step away. It was far too tempting to stay where she was and hibernate within the cocoon of his consideration. 'I'll see you in the morning,' she murmured as she opened the car door and slid into her seat, when all she wanted to do was walk back to him and wrap her arms around him in the hope that he would wrap his around her.

'Idiot!' she berated herself as she made her way down the hill, passing the turning that would have taken her towards Penhally Bay Surgery and the lifeboat station until she came to her grandmother's cottage.

She switched off the engine then realised that she would far rather turn round and drive back up the hill than go into the darkened house that had been a haven for most of her life. It seemed somehow sad and abandoned now that she knew Beabea wasn't in there waiting to hear about her day; now that she knew that her grandmother would never be coming back to her little cottage again.

Zayed made one last soft-footed tour through the house as everyone settled down for the night, wondering idly what its wealthy former owner would make of the place.

The basic structure was unchanged, but where the rooms had looked spacious and luxurious before, now some of them almost resembled a cross between boarding-school dormitories and an old-fashioned hospital ward, albeit one with all the latest high-tech gadgetry.

The kitchen where he'd helped himself to a last cup of wickedly strong coffee could have rivalled the best in any of the local hotels and…

'Stop wasting time,' he growled into the silence of the one room that was exclusively his as he leant wearily back against the door. 'There is no point in trying to picture the place through her eyes. She has already told you that she is impressed. And as for the way she was with the children…'

That was the biggest problem, he admitted honestly. The children.

There had been something that had felt so *right* when the two of them had been sharing the storytelling this evening. It had felt to him almost as if they had been playacting at being parents, and he could see that it had been affecting her every bit as much. And when he had sensed how reluctant she had been to leave…

'That can*not* be allowed to happen,' he growled fiercely as he kicked off his soft shoes and padded barefoot across the emptiness of the sparsely furnished room towards the bed. 'She is a talented doctor who could go far. She does not need any involvement in my life, except as a member of staff.'

But even though he said the words aloud, it didn't stop the thoughts from circling inside his head. Like the intriguing fact that she might be a highly intelligent and dedicated doctor with a lovely rapport with children of all ages, but it almost seemed as if in other ways she was an innocent.

It was all too easy to remember the smiles she'd bestowed on Abir and their other little charges at St Piran's, and Leela and the others this evening, but it was also dangerously easy to imagine them being directed his way as he discovered exactly what it would take to make her pulse race and the stunning green of her eyes darken with arousal.

'As if that could ever happen!' he scoffed bitterly, dismissing the impossible image of Emily Livingston cradling a dark-haired baby against the pale skin of her breast and smiling up at him as the greedy mouth suckled her.

'Been there, done that,' he whispered, with a pang of renewed agony for everything he'd lost, knowing that he could never replace it.

And that was why there was absolutely no point in allowing himself to dream that Emily could ever be a permanent part of his life. There was no way he could ask her to give up her obvious natural desire for eventual motherhood, even if he could guarantee her safety, and there was no way he could ever allow himself to be the cause of her destruction.

He already had far too much blood on his hands.

CHAPTER SEVEN

SOMETHING had changed, but she had no idea why.

Emily clicked her safety belt in position and started the engine before she leant back in her seat and stared up at Zayed's house thoughtfully, trying to pinpoint what was different and when it had happened.

It was nearly a week since that first visit to his house but the magical feeling of being somehow connected to the man may as well have been the last remembered wisps of a dream for all the evidence she'd seen of it since then.

Oh, she was made perfectly welcome by everyone else, and gave them all endless entertainment as she tried to learn enough of their language to be able to communicate in the simplest way with them. Her story-telling was much in demand, too, but, much to her disappointment, since that first day Zayed's role as interpreter had been taken over by Reza or one of the other staff.

In fact, it was almost as if Zayed was deliberately distancing himself from her, just when she'd realised...

'Oh, damn!' Emily breathed when the enormity of her feelings suddenly overwhelmed her.

All she had to do was picture the first moment she'd

seen Zayed—the handsome man she'd watched smiling down at Abir—or recall his delighted grin when he'd been submerged under a pile of wriggling children, or the gentle concern he'd shown for Beabea, to know that she *had* completely lost her heart.

'I'm in love with him,' she whispered, saying those special words aloud for the very first time in her life.

And now that she'd made the admission, simple honesty meant that she would also have to admit that the feeling had been growing with every day they worked together and with every new facet she discovered of this complex man's personality.

Unfortunately, that same honesty compelled her to acknowledge that the emotion would be completely wasted on the man because there was so little chance that her feelings would be returned. It wouldn't matter how much she loved him or for how long because it just wasn't going to be reciprocated, not while he was haunted by shadows from his past.

Whatever had happened in his former life to drive him out of his own country seemed to have been dreadful enough to close off the essential part of him that would ever be able to love her in return.

Emily put the car in gear and set off down the driveway with a heavy heart.

It would have been wonderful if the realisation that she'd finally fallen in love could be accompanied with the knowledge that she was loved in return, but that wasn't the case.

Zayed Khalil might be—*was*—the embodiment of everything she'd ever dreamed of in a life's partner... hard working, honest, intelligent, handsome, caring... but the last few days had confirmed, without a word needing to be spoken, that he was interested in only one thing—operating on his little patients and seeing them returned to their parents whole and healthy.

Just this week, Emily had assisted while he'd done his utmost to correct clubbed feet that should have been dealt with years earlier, and had given a new cheekbone and eye socket, to replace one eaten away by disease, to a little girl who had believed she would always be too ugly to have any friends.

She'd been given an enormous boost in confidence when he'd offered a quiet word of approval when she'd closed at the end of a particularly harrowing mixed-discipline operation to repair the results of a child on a bicycle who had strayed into the path of a reversing tractor, but as she let herself into Beabea's darkened cottage it was time for her to admit the painful truth.

She may be the important second pair of hands when she was with him at the operating table, and the second pair of eyes when they were checking on the patients in post-op and ICU, but she could just as well be a particularly sophisticated robot for all the response Zayed had to her on a personal level.

'Did I do something wrong?' she murmured as she stood in front of the fridge and tried to summon up some enthusiasm for eating.

If anything, she would have expected him to withdraw from her after she'd worked on his painful muscles and ligaments down on the beach. If he was going to distance himself from her, that would have been the one time that she'd obviously stepped over the boundaries between his exalted status and her far lowlier one.

And yet… She shook her head when she realised that he hadn't completely withdrawn from all contact with her because Beabea had told her that he'd been back several times to visit her.

At first, Emily had wondered if the visits had been a figment of her grandmother's mind under the influence of the strong painkillers, but when Nick Tremayne had mentioned bumping into her boss the last time she'd encountered him at Beabea's bedside, she'd realised that it must be true.

So why would he visit an elderly lady in the final stages of terminal cancer while he avoided spending any but the most essential time with her granddaughter?

Unless... An awful thought suddenly made her feel so ill that she abandoned the sandwich she'd just constructed as though it was contaminated with deadly bacteria.

Had she inadvertently revealed the strength of her feelings towards him? Had he realised that she was falling in love with him before even she had recognised it? Had he been so horrified by the unwelcome thought that he'd immediately done the only thing available to him—put as much distance between them as possible?

Her face felt hot with embarrassment but her body was cold and clammy as though she was going into shock.

What could she do about the situation to make it less...uncomfortable?

'Well, resigning isn't an option,' she said aloud, and found her determination bolstered by hearing the words. 'I'm not doing anything that might make visiting Beabea any more complicated. And, anyway, I like the job and I know I'm learning so much from him.'

That was one thing she *could* admit—Zayed was a

generous and gifted teacher, probably one of the best she'd had since she'd started her medical training.

'And I'm pathetic,' she admitted softly, not liking the truth of those words quite so much. 'He obviously doesn't want any sort of relationship with me beyond our professional one, but I still want to be near him.'

So, how was she going to deal with the situation?

'Well, I'm certainly not going to be skulking around in the shadows to stay out of his sight,' she said firmly. 'I am who I am, and if he doesn't like it, tough!'

She would still be doing her work to the best of her ability and she had no intention of cutting back on her visits to the children and staff at his house. And as for her visits to the beach…?

'Well, it was *my* beach before it was his,' she said, then giggled when she realised just how childish that sounded.

But it was true. She'd been going to that beach ever since she'd come to live with Beabea, and no taciturn surgeon was going to drive her away.

'Besides, if he insists on going swimming when there's no one else about to keep an eye on his safety, then he's just going to have to put up with me being there.' And it would be her private, guilty pleasure to look at that taut, tanned body and dream of what might have been, if only…

Anyway, the trips to the beach would end soon enough. They were halfway through September already, and the evenings were starting to draw in. All too soon it would be dark by the time they finished work at St Piran's and made the journey across to the coast to Penhally, and she didn't think that even Zayed would be foolish enough to swim alone in the dark in winter.

'And if he tries it, I'll bring Beabea's big torch down and use it like the lifeboat men's searchlight,' she declared, just before a jaw-cracking yawn overtook her.

It didn't take long to get ready for bed, but even when she was comfortably ensconced with a large mug of hot chocolate and a fresh sandwich, her brain wouldn't let the topic go.

All she had to do was think about seeing Zayed in the unit the next morning and a whole squadron of butterflies tried to steal her appetite.

'Enough of this nonsense!' she said, drawing on the determination that had got her through the first crippling weeks of loneliness when she'd left the cosy familiar world of Penhally for medical school, and had fired her to do her utmost to make her grandmother proud of her.

'First of all, much as it injures my pride and my heart, I've got to accept that there's never going to be anything personal between us.' The bald words *did* hurt, but they were necessary if she was going to be able to do her job properly.

'Secondly…what?' She took a bite of her sandwich and savoured the tang of the locally made cheese complemented to perfection with slices of the last of Beabea's home-grown tomatoes. The only thing that could have made it better was if it had been between two slices of Beabea's home-made bread, but that was already a thing of the past.

Tears burned her eyes but she refused to let them fall. There would be plenty of time for that later, when the worst finally happened. For now, it was important that she work out what sort of relationship she could have with Zayed as the one she wanted was impossible.

'Friends?' she suggested tentatively, and paused while the idea grew like a plant from a single tiny seed. 'Yes. Why not friends?' The word wasn't nearly so tentative the second time as she visualised a return of the fledgling camaraderie that had been such a good part of their first few days of working together.

Was it possible?

'Well, I won't know unless I try,' she declared, and smiled when she heard an echo of Beabea's voice in the words.

She was still smiling when she turned out the light and settled under the covers, comforted by the realisation that for the rest of her life there would be moments when advice her grandmother had given her or even just a turn of phrase would bring memories of the wonderful woman back to her.

It would never be the same as having her grandmother there in her life, but at least it wouldn't feel as if she'd lost her completely.

The next morning Emily implemented her plan, breezing into the unit with a cheery greeting for each member of staff she encountered.

'Shirley! I love the new hairstyle,' she said to Zayed's new secretary, meaning every word of it. The motherly woman was one of the old school, and had apparently been letting herself slide slowly towards retirement until she'd been sent at short notice to replace Nasima Osman, when her predecessor had been fired and sent back to Xandar.

It was amazing what difference a few days of working for someone who appreciated her meticulous approach to her job had made to her…or was it the fact that Zayed's dark eyes lighting up his handsome face had reminded her that she wasn't just a secretary but a woman, too?

'Good morning, Zayed,' she said equally cheerfully, even though the fact that he'd refused to meet her eyes had embedded the barb of disappointment a little deeper in her heart. 'How was Reza's migraine? Did the tablets work for her?'

She hardly left him enough time to confirm that Reza was back on form before she was off again and hailing the children's favourite staff nurse. 'Jenna, how did the birthday party go? Was Steve surprised when he found the whole family there?'

Emily was relieved when Jenna drew her along to the office to check some details in a file, chattering all the while about the surprise party she'd arranged for her husband's birthday. She didn't think she could have kept the 'bright and breezy' front up for very much longer knowing that a certain pair of dark eyes were boring into her back with an all-too-familiar intensity. She could almost hear his thoughts as he registered the fact that she was behaving differently, today. Perhaps he was trying to work it all out, to decide what she was up to.

'Well, let him wonder,' she said under her breath as another busy shift got under way. 'He's made it clear that he's not interested in being a lover or a husband, but that doesn't mean that I can't have him as a friend.'

'Abir looks so much better today,' Emily said to the Hananis, laboriously trying out one of the sentences she'd been taught last night.

And it was true. He did look much better, the swelling around his eyes all but gone and his mischievous nature already asserting itself.

In fact, if it weren't for the thick protective bandages still swathed around his head, you would hardly know that the little boy would have had no chance of a normal life before he'd come into Zayed's care at St Piran's Hospital.

'How he is looking is no much important,' Meera Hanani said fiercely, trying out some of the English she'd been equally determined to learn. 'Abir is my son, so he always look good to me. Now his head is good, too, *everything* is good.'

A little gurgle drew their attention down to the bright eyes twinkling up at them and the gummy grin that had become a permanent feature since he'd recovered from the immediate trauma of the operation.

'Yes, it is good,' Emily agreed. 'But now he looks like his daddy again, so this is good too.'

'Very good,' Meera agreed with a shy smile in Athar's direction. She said something to her husband in their own language but it was spoken far too quickly for Emily to understand with her limited vocabulary. Whatever it was, the two of them shared a soft-eyed smile before Meera turned to her and continued. 'We have a baby again.'

Emily frowned slightly, not quite certain what she meant. Was she saying that she felt as if Abir was theirs again?

'More baby,' Meera said, and touched a hand to her waist, and Emily felt the smile bloom across her face.

'Congratulations, both of you!' she exclaimed in delight, spontaneously wrapping an arm around each of them. 'I'm so happy for you.'

It was only later, when she was sitting surrounded by several piles of paperwork, that she allowed herself to explore the sudden pang of jealousy that had struck her when she'd heard the Hananis' news.

It was crazy for her to feel envious of them after all they'd been through in the last couple of months. They were due for a bit of good news, and she really was delighted for them, but...

'Has my biological clock suddenly started ticking?' she wondered, only realising that she'd voiced the question aloud when Jenna answered her.

'Working with Zayed Khalil is enough to get anyone's biological clock ticking.' She laughed. 'Isn't he just the sexiest man you've ever met?'

'Sexier than Colin Firth in Pride and Prejudice?' Emily challenged, knowing from a previous conversation that he was one of Jenna's all-time favourite actors and hoping desperately that she wasn't blushing.

'Ah! Now you're talking!' the staff nurse sighed then looked thoughtful. 'Actually, they both have that same dark brooding quality to them, and the feeling that, once they fall in love, there's nothing they wouldn't do for the woman in their life.'

'And does your Steve know you feel like this?' Emily teased. 'Doesn't he feel jealous?'

'Nah!' Jenna laughed. 'He knows that I might go starry-eyed over some actor—or our illustrious consultant—but Steve's the one I go to bed with.'

'So he's confident you're not pining for the unobtainable?' Unlike me, she added silently.

'Definitely not pining,' Jenna said with a saucy wink. 'How about you?'

Could the woman read her mind? Was it obvious to everyone that she'd fallen in love with Zayed? Would the gossip be all around the hospital by lunchtime?

'Colin Firth's OK, I suppose. He's a pretty good actor, and he was just right as Mr Darcy, but he doesn't really ring any bells for me,' she invented hastily, knowing that any slight of her hero would distract Jenna from pursuing the topic in Zayed's direction.

'*OK?* He's far more than OK,' she said as she sniffed in disgust and sailed out of the room. 'Some people just don't have any taste' was her parting shot as the door swung shut behind her.

'Oh, but they do,' Emily murmured softly as she forced her eyes back to the open file in front of her, in spite of the image of Zayed imprinted in her brain. 'Impeccable taste.'

'Is there a problem?' the man in question asked, and Emily found herself fighting a blush again. Rather than turning towards him and have him question the heat in her face, she focused on the information she was adding to Abir's file.

'It's not a problem yet, but it's something that will need to be checked in about nine months' time,' she said as she completed her notes.

'Nine months? That is very specific,' he commented as he hitched one hip on the corner of the table. 'So, what is it that will need investigation?'

'Read for yourself,' she said, and handed him the file with a smile, looking forward to seeing his delight.

Except it wasn't delight that crossed his face when

he read the fact that Meera Hanani was pregnant again. It looked far more like…pain.

And then the expression was gone, wiped away as if it had never appeared, leaving the stoic, apparently emotionless man behind.

'I will make sure that the baby can be checked after it is born,' he said flatly, without any evidence of pleasure in the young couple's news, and Emily couldn't help staring at him in consternation. This wasn't the same man who had smiled down at Abir that first morning, or the one who had allowed the children to swarm all over him as soon as he'd set foot inside his house.

What on earth had happened since then to change him so much? And how could she ever ask him?

Once again, the answer came down to friendship, she decided as she swiftly stripped off her clothes to don theatre scrubs a little later. If she could show him that being friends wasn't a threat— could even be enjoyable—then perhaps he would relax enough to tell her about the demons that beset him.

'Our patient is Raquia Khan,' Zayed said to the assembled staff as soon as she joined him at the table, and despite the fact that he was all professional detachment, just the sound of his voice was enough to send a shiver up her spine. 'Raquia is a twin. The delivery of her brother was straightforward but Raquia suffered considerable trauma due to malpresentation, receiving a broken clavicle…' He stroked the slightly misshapen collar-bone with a gloved finger and Emily couldn't take her eyes off the gentle movement '…and a broken radius and ulna.'

It was obvious that both bones in the little forearm

were considerably deformed, as though they had simply been left to heal without being positioned correctly.

'Unfortunately, the injuries were apparently completely overlooked by the midwife, who was more concerned with the survival of the mother and her son.' There was an edge to his voice as he recounted the details and Emily was glad to hear it—it was proof that he wasn't as detached as he would have them think. But was it enough to allow herself to hope that she might be able to get through to him?

'This has left Raquia without the full range of rotational movement in her arm as the bones cannot slide properly past each other,' he continued after a moment, once more the cool, calm professional. 'Today we will re-break both bones in her arm and position them correctly, using titanium screws and plates where necessary. Because this arm is considerably shorter than the other, we may have to use bone grafts to fill in and speed up the repair process, but this should not be difficult.'

'Won't there be a problem with her skin?' asked one of the newer trainee theatre staff, her face almost purple with embarrassment as everyone looked across at her. 'Will it stretch enough for you to lengthen it that far?'

'That is a good question,' Zayed said with a smile that was evident even behind the camouflaging mask, immediately putting her at ease. 'In some cases—for example, a little boy we had in the unit a couple of months ago—we would have to attach the two ends of the bone to a frame and wind them apart day by day to lengthen the bone gradually to the right length. With Raquia that will not be necessary because, although the difference looks great, it is not too far for her skin to accommodate.'

'How do you know?' Emily was beginning to suspect that the young trainee was deliberately attracting Zayed's attention to herself...or was that her own jealousy talking?

'Obviously, I wasn't given green eyes without a reason,' she muttered under her breath, glad that her mask disguised the fact that she was speaking...except when she glanced up it was to see a pair of dark eyes watching her intently, with a hint of a smile in their glittering depths.

'Years of experience tell me so,' Zayed answered. 'But that does not mean that sometimes we do not have to change what we intend to do when we start the operation. So, if we need to use a fixator, we will do so, but I do not expect it will be necessary today.'

And he was right in his assessment. Raquia's surgery went as smoothly as anyone could have wished, and although her arm looked badly bruised by the end of the operation and would look even worse during the next couple of days, that would be largely hidden from view by the dressings. Then, once the stitches were ready for removal, any residual discolouration would have time to disappear by the time the full cast was removed.

'If you would like to close, Emily, I will go to talk to the parents of Raquia.'

Emily was becoming quite accustomed to being left to complete the process and took it as a mark of his confidence in her growing skills that he would sometimes even leave the room for a short while. In this case, she could understand that he would want to put Raquia's parents' minds at rest. They had been feeling so guilty that their daughter hadn't received the care she'd needed, even though they had a ready-made excuse in the fact that they lived so many miles from the nearest hospital.

Zayed left the room on silent feet and as Emily bent to her task, she wondered if she was the only one who had noticed that he had performed more than half of the surgery without his clogs on. He certainly seemed to be less uncomfortable during the more lengthy procedures these days, but whether that was due to her suggestion that he go barefoot or proof that his injuries were finally improving was something else she couldn't ask him—at least, not unless they were friends rather than professional colleagues.

'Have you been to see your grandmother this evening?'

Zayed's husky voice reached Emily over the rhythmic flow and hiss of the waves across the silvery sand but she wasn't surprised to hear him speak. She seemed to have developed some sort of sixth sense that told her whenever he was nearby, and even though she hadn't seen him come onto the beach, she'd somehow known he was there. She wasn't even surprised that he'd learned how to find her secret thinking place among the jumbled rocks.

'I went as soon as I got to Penhally,' she confirmed with a brief glance in his direction, her spirits the lowest they'd ever been. 'She was asleep when I got there and only woke up for a few minutes before she dropped off again.'

'Is this not what you would want?' he asked softly, perching on a nearby rock as though prepared to stay for a while. 'Would you prefer that she was awake and in pain?'

'No! No, of course I wouldn't,' she protested, then flung up her hands. 'Oh, just ignore me. I'm feeling disgustingly sorry for myself. I should be glad that she's not in any discomfort and all I can do is complain that she's not alert enough to talk to me.'

'But this is understandable, too,' he said, his soft words eddying around the two of them in the fitful breeze. 'You have the feeling of time running out and the need to hear any last words of wisdom, the need to hear once more that you are loved and to say that you love in return.'

'That's exactly the way it is. How did you know?' she demanded.

'I lost my grandmother, too, and I can remember.' There was a slightly hollow sound to his voice, as though part of him was lost in thoughts and memories.

'It is the ones you lose without warning that are worst,' he added suddenly, almost as though the words had been torn out of him against his will. 'Then there is no chance to apologise for the things you failed to do, no time for a final declaration of love.'

He shook himself, as though suddenly realising where he was and who he was speaking to, and stood up.

'I came to deliver an invitation,' he said formally. 'It is the birthday of Jasmine Mohatar and she has asked if you will come to take a piece of birthday cake with us. And Reza has said that *I* will get no cake if I do not bring you.'

Emily laughed aloud. She could just imagine Reza

delivering that sort of ultimatum, despite the fact that Zayed was her employer.

'I would be delighted to have some of Jasmine's cake. How is her spine progressing?' It was the first time Emily had ever seen TB in a spine, outside pictures in medical textbooks, and she'd quickly realised just how vital it was to support the weakened structure during the treatment phase so that it wouldn't collapse before new bone could be laid down.

'There will be no miracles in one night,' he said as the two of them set off across the sand towards the steps that led to the car park at the top of the cliff. 'As you know, the treatment of the tuberculosis will take a year or more, and it will take at least that long for her body to grow new bone.'

'How much longer will she stay in Penhally? Does she need to be over here the whole time she's in treatment and recovery?' She could only imagine how disruptive that would be to the rest of the Mohatar family. So far, every member who'd been tested to see if they, too, had TB, had been negative, but all their lives must have been thrown into disorder when Jasmine had needed to come to Penhally for the treatment she'd needed.

On a purely practical level, it was much more difficult to deal with Jasmine than most of the other patients due to the infectious nature of the disease she'd contracted. And barrier nursing was time-consuming and could end up being costly…although she knew that Zayed wouldn't let that be a consideration. As far as he was concerned, the only criterion would be that none of the other patients should be put at risk while he completed Jasmine's treatment.

'I have been in contact with an old colleague in Xandar,' Zayed said, and she noticed that his accent became just a little stronger when he spoke of his own country.

Was there also a hint of longing in his voice?

Did he miss the familiar heat and the sights and sounds he'd grown up with?

Were there people he was longing to see?

Would he eventually leave Cornwall to return there, leaving others to continue his work at St Piran's and at his house on the outskirts of Penhally, leaving her to mourn the man she'd never forget?

'If I can set everything up, he will supervise the continuing treatment of Jasmine when she returns to Xandar, and will send me reports of her progress. That way, she will be close to her family and will be able to see her brothers so she does not become a stranger to them.'

'How soon will she be able to go?' Emily asked eagerly. 'She was in tears today because her baby brother has learned to walk while she's been away and she missed seeing it, and now it's her birthday and she can't share her cake with them.'

'She will probably be able to leave by the end of the week, if all goes well, but her parents must be willing to take her for her treatment without fail, or the TB may become resistant.'

'Well, if you speak to the father while I take the mother to one side, we should be able to impress on each of them how deadly that could be...for the whole family.'

She stood aside while he unlocked his car then slid onto the supple leather seat, slightly disappointed that there would be no leisurely walk along Harbour Road to get to his usual parking place. Making the journey by car left her with far too little time to spend with him, especially if she was going to try to find ways to build a friendship between the two of them.

'How is your own back these days?' she asked, as a tentative idea began to form.

'A little better, thank you,' he said, politeness itself.

'Good enough to go surfing?' she suggested, as she hid her superstitiously crossed fingers under the folds of her skirt.

'*Surfing?* I do not think so,' he said, clearly appalled by the idea.

'You make it sound as if I'd invited you to parade along Harbour Road naked!' she teased. 'What's wrong with surfing? It's done all around the world by everyone from little children to their grandparents. *I* do it, too.'

'I do not think this would be appropriate,' he demurred. 'I have seen the people who surf during the summer with their baggy, garish clothing and their—'

'Oh, don't be so stuffy, Zayed!' she broke in impatiently. 'Relax a bit and enjoy life. If you were any stiffer, I could use *you* as a surfboard.'

CHAPTER EIGHT

STIFF enough to use as a surfboard? If only that were true, Zayed thought bitterly.

Ever since the explosion there had been what his consultant had euphemistically called 'no activity' in that important part of his male anatomy.

Was it a fitting punishment for his failures as a husband?

Perhaps.

But it was just one more reason why he could never allow anything personal to develop between himself and Emily, no matter how much his soul yearned for just a little of her sunshine in his life.

At first his surgeon had thought that his inability to perform was the result of his traumatic injuries, especially when he'd spent several days convinced that the paralysis was going to be permanent. But then he'd regained the use of his legs and the man had been distraught to have to tell him that he had absolutely no idea why the rest of his system hadn't returned to normal function.

The thud of Emily's car door closing snapped him out of his useless musings and he followed her to the front door.

'They here!' shrieked one little voice, and the mayhem that announcement caused was instantaneous.

He was aware that Emily wisely stood aside while he allowed himself to be besieged by all those eager little recuperating bodies, carefully staging his spectacular fall so that none of the children was bumped or jostled.

As if they would care! All they were interested in was seeing how many of them could sit on his chest or any other part of his anatomy they could pin down while he pretended to struggle mightily.

And all the time he was overwhelmingly aware that Emily was watching everything that was going on.

What was she thinking?

Was her attention nothing more than concern that he might cause a setback in one of the children's recovery? Was she dismayed that he could so easily abandon the proper gravitas of his position?

A quick glance in her direction between the flailing limbs told him that this, at least, wasn't true, not if the wistful smile was any indication. She looked almost as if she would like to join in the mêlée, or…or what?

Suddenly he wasn't quite so sure that he'd been making the right decisions in his life recently, and it was all the fault of this beautiful woman.

Oh, he knew that there could never be anything sexual between them, but what if she could accept…?

No! It wouldn't be fair to ask her to condemn herself to a life without bearing children. She would be so good at loving them and taking care of them. And he already knew, from meeting her grandmother, that Emily wasn't the sort of woman to be satisfied with anything less than the dreams she'd set her heart on.

That meant that offering her nothing more than friendship would be…

'Impossible!' he declared aloud, and startled the giggling children into wary silence.

'You are all impossible,' he said, this time with what he hoped was a wolfish grin as he pretended to take bites out of each of them. 'And now it is time for you to get ready for bed.'

'Not bed. Story first!' declared an emphatic little voice, and this time his grin was genuine.

'OK, Leela. Story it is,' he conceded when they all joined in the demand, and sighed with relief when the last little body crawled off him.

'Are you all right?' That could only be Emily's voice, filled with concern, as was the hand that she offered to help him lever himself to his feet. It was such a slender, soft little hand but already showing the skill that would make her a superb surgeon…and with enough hidden strength to counteract the weight of a full-grown man.

'I am all right,' he confirmed, his voice sharper than it should have been as he tried to ignore the urge to hang onto that brief connection.

'I was only concerned that the children might have hurt you,' she explained quietly, and he realised that even though she clearly thought he was rebuffing her concern, she was keeping her voice below the level of volume of the children's excited chatter. 'The children are getting stronger and fitter—and putting on weight and muscle with all the physiotherapy and special food they're getting—and they might not realise that they were—'

'It is all right Emily,' he soothed, and allowed himself a brief touch of her hand. 'I understand what you are saying, but I was not hurt. Rather, it is I who worry that I might hurt them.'

Her smile made his heart kick hard in his chest. 'You would never hurt a child,' she declared confidently. 'In fact, I've never met a man who would make a more perfect father. Reza thinks you should have a whole houseful of children of your own.'

Her praise was like a kick to another portion of his anatomy and all the more painful for the knowledge that it wasn't true...could never be true.

'Not so,' he said gruffly, the words having to be forced from his throat with the realisation that it was time for an overdue conversation.

The situation had never arisen before because he'd never allowed any of his other colleagues to get past their professional relationship, but there had been something different about Emily right from the first time he'd set eyes on her.

And just now there had been a light in her eyes and a lightening in her voice that had told him she wasn't any more immune to it than he was, but it couldn't go on, couldn't go any further, not when there was no future in it for either of them.

'I need to speak to you,' he said, and only realised how grim he'd sounded when he saw the worried way her eyes widened, their soothing green darkening with concern.

'Of course,' she said, her voice calm in spite of the fact that he knew from the frantic pounding at her slender throat that her pulse rate had just doubled. 'When? In the morning at the hospital?'

That would be the more professional choice. It would help him to put a necessary distance between them, but the morning was far too many sleepless hours away. Perhaps, once he'd told her the whole dreadful story, she would stop haunting his dreams.

'No. Tonight,' he decided, 'after the children have had their story.'

He silently cursed his own cowardice, but he wanted to have one last happy memory to counteract the terrible emptiness that would be left once he'd pushed her completely out of his life.

It would be better for both of them if he could dismiss her from the unit, too, but that was impossible. Not only did he need her growing skill to achieve what he wanted for their little charges, but he wouldn't do something so destructive to her career. She didn't deserve it, not when any problems between them were his fault.

'Come in,' he invited an hour later after a story time that had been, if anything, more fun than ever before. Had that been because he knew it was probably the last?

Zayed turned to close the door behind her and surprised a look of blank shock on Emily's face as she took her first look around his private space.

He scanned the room and only then realised just what a bleak place it was.

There was a bed, of course, and a wardrobe for his clothing, and a desk for his computer, which was liberally piled with paperwork, but apart from that virtually nothing, certainly nothing decorative—no little oasis of exotic sun-baked Xandar transported to a Cornish cliff-top home or anything of a personal nature—and having seen her grandmother's collection of family photos, he knew instinctively that those were what she'd been expecting to see.

'Would you prefer to take the chair by the desk or

sit on the bed?' Those were the only two options in his barren private space and he cursed at the way his own pulse responded to the wash of colour that swept up her face when she glanced at the place where he slept. With difficulty, he forced himself to focus on the fact that the blush only went to confirm his initial assessment of her—that even at thirty years of age she wasn't the sort of woman who was accustomed to spending much time in men's bedrooms.

'Um, the chair, please,' she said, and scurried across to stake her claim.

He almost smiled at the way she avoided looking at his bed, but that was the only light moment there could be in this room. By the time he'd finished talking to her, he'd be surprised if she even wanted to stay on his team, no matter how much damage it would do to her career.

But where to start?

He'd never spoken to anyone in Cornwall about what had happened in Xandar and it was almost impossible now to separate the events from the terrible guilt and the pain of loss.

'Why don't you have any photos of your family?' Emily asked, then bit her lip as though worried that she'd overstepped the invisible boundaries he'd set up around himself. He could have blessed her for supplying him with the perfect place to start his confession.

'Because…they remind me,' he said haltingly, any fluency gone as he tried to find the words to explain the inexplicable. 'And it is already hard enough, living with the memories.'

'But that's what they're for…so that you don't forget

all the happy times,' she said eagerly, and he almost resented her for her naiveté.

'Even if the memories are of guilt and loss?' he demanded harshly. 'Even if all they remind you of is the fact that, once upon a time, you had everything you could want and you had been so careless of it that you had lost it all?'

The memories were all around him now—no need for photographs—and he could almost hear the screams and smell the tang of blood under the choking blanket of explosives and dust.

'It was my job to protect them,' he said, barely aware that she was there and yet knowing that he had to continue so that she would know…would know everything. 'I should have stopped her from being there, from bringing him with her…especially when there had been so many warnings. But she was so determined to be there for the opening ceremony…said that after all the hours it had taken me away from my family she had a *right* to be there…'

He shook his head, unable to continue, and to his horror felt the swift slide of tears down his face.

Embarrassed by his lack of control, he whirled away from her and dragged both hands over his face but that couldn't stop them now that the dam had been breached.

'I am sorry for this,' he muttered brokenly, but he needn't have bothered because suddenly she was there, right in front of him, and in her eyes he saw not condemnation or pity but a deep well of empathy that he would never deserve.

'Sit down,' she urged, guiding him to the bed she'd rejected just a few minutes ago, then stood close be-

side him and cradled his head against her as though
he were one of the children now sleeping peacefully
around them.

It took some time before the heart-wrenching sobs finally died away but Emily still hadn't worked out the
best way to approach their aftermath.

Like any proud man, Zayed would be mortified to
have broken down in front of her unless she handled
the situation just right.

But what *was* just right?

She had so little experience that she could very well
make everything much worse, especially as she had
little idea what had actually happened. His words had
been so broken, wrenched out of the nightmare scenes
playing inside his head. All she was really certain of
was that he'd lost his family in some disaster and was
convinced that it had been his fault that they'd died.

Well, the only way to be sure that she wasn't going
to rip open even more wounds was to wait until he'd
recovered himself and ask him to explain.

'I'm sorry,' he said hoarsely. 'That was not supposed
to happen.' He tried to pull away from her but she deliberately tightened her arm around his shoulders.

'There's no need to apologise for tears,' she said
firmly. 'They're just a physiological fact of life, like
sneezing or yawning. A manifestation of the body's
need for some sort of cathartic release that—'

'All right, Emily, thank you for the lecture, but—'

'But I need to know something,' she interrupted
quickly, afraid that if she gave him too much time he'd
retire behind those barricades that kept the world at bay.
'What happened? Down on the beach you said it was

an explosion that caused your injuries, but you didn't say what caused the explosion. Was it during an earthquake, or some other sort of disaster?'

'Would that it had been something as innocent as an earthquake,' he said, and drew in a shuddering sigh before sitting silent for so long that she began to think he'd changed his mind about talking to her.

Finally, he tipped his face up to hers and she could have cried herself when she saw the mixture of pain and guilt that dulled his eyes.

'If you want to hear the whole depressing story, you had better sit down,' he suggested wearily, and gestured towards the almost clinically neat bedding beside him. 'It is not something that can be done in a moment or two.'

He seemed so reluctant that she almost offered to leave instead, but something inside her knew that he needed the relief of speaking about what had happened. And if he regretted it in the morning, he could always console himself that she would be leaving in a matter of months.

'In Xandar, my family is…powerful,' he began, and as ever when he spoke of his home country she noticed that his accent grew stronger, the syllables flowing like exotic honey from his tongue. 'Even before I started my medical training it was obvious that the poorer people did not have access to the medical services they needed for their children. So I was determined to build a place where specialist doctors could come from many countries to treat the children who had no help and teach us what we needed to know about their care.'

'Like the one at St Piran's? A special unit that can

call on all the different specialties within the hospital, depending on the needs of a particular patient?'

'Exactly so. It was the unit I planned in Xandar on which my department at St Piran's is based. Unfortunately,' he continued, with a visible darkening of his expression, 'there are in my country some who would keep things as they have always been and who refuse to accept that modern medicine—even when it is delivered by women—is a good thing.'

'And your unit was actually built?' He'd said something about an opening ceremony, so...

'Not only the unit,' he said with a hint of pride, 'but also the start of a series of clinics throughout the country so that little ones could be seen more quickly and easily than having to travel all the way to the capital. Then only if an operation was necessary would the family have the expense of that journey.'

'And the explosion?' She hated to push him to recall such distressing events, but she was discovering that she needed to know what had happened to the man she loved every bit as much as he needed to tell her.

'The world believes that it was caused by a group of rabid fundamentalists—those who object to all things that come from outside the traditions of our country.'

'But?' It was anger she had heard in his voice just then, fierce and raw.

'None of these groups claimed responsibility for the atrocity, the way they usually do, and there were other people who had their own reasons...' He shook his head. 'It is complicated...politics...but I believe that it was someone who used the threats by the fundamentalists to hide their own agenda. And they almost succeeded...

except *I* didn't die. It was my wife and son who were destroyed because I didn't protect them.'

'*Didn't* protect them or *couldn't* protect them?' she asked, remembering the fact that he'd been badly injured, too.

'There can be no difference because I failed them. They died that day and I lived,' he said, voicing the torment that sounded as if it would never leave him.

It was almost as though a light bulb switched on inside her head.

'And is this why you hold yourself aloof from everyone...why you won't let anyone get close to you?'

'Why would anyone want to?' he asked, those broad shoulders slumping in the closest she'd ever seen him come to defeat. 'I am a man who has nothing to give... who deserves nothing...because I have not proved myself worthy.'

Those lean fingers she'd watched, mesmerised while they'd performed their magic for his little patients, were knotted into white-knuckled fists now.

Emily wanted so very much to reach across and soothe those fists with gentle fingers, but she knew he was in no mood to accept such a gesture from her.

'So, in Xandar there's no such thing as someone being granted a second chance?' she asked quietly, knowing he was intelligent enough to get her point.

'Of course there is, if the person deserves a second chance,' he retorted. 'But how can I have a second chance when they never will?' His dark eyes almost burned her with their intensity as he continued.

'Leika was twenty-four when she died, young and beautiful and with so much life in her.'

'Leika?' Jealousy sank its claws deep into her soul.

'Zuleika,' he clarified. 'She was my wife, chosen for me by my family to cement a political alliance, and the price I had to pay for agreement to my plan for the specialist unit.'

The fact that Zayed was important enough to Xandar that he could be coerced into such a match was almost irrelevant to Emily when all she felt was a selfish relief that it hadn't been a love match between them.

'Neither of us really wanted to marry,' he continued in a low voice full of regret. 'Leika wanted to pursue a career in law, specialising in what are called *women's issues*, so when Kashif was born a year later, she almost resented him because everyone expected her to do the traditional thing...the *right* thing...and give up her work to stay home with him.'

'So when the unit was going to open—the unit that her marriage had allowed—she was determined to be there,' Emily said, reading between the lines.

'And when the explosion came, I couldn't save them.' His dark eyes were full of torment as they stared right through her, and she knew that he was seeing the horrors in his memory instead. 'I'm a doctor but I couldn't do anything for them. I just...just lay there and watched them die, right in front of me.'

Probably because you were too badly injured to get to them, she reflected, knowing with absolute certainty that he would have done everything in his power to help them if he'd been able.

Not that she could say any of that, she knew as she allowed her eyes to drift around his room again.

The barrenness of his surroundings was still a shock. When he'd invited her into his private space, she'd been expecting to see a little bit of Xandar transported to

Penhally. Fabrics with a rich variety of textures and colours, perhaps even the luxury of silk on his bed. She certainly hadn't imagined this…this monk's cell.

And when she'd mentioned the lack of family photos, she'd actually seen him shut down to avoid the pain, but hadn't known why until now.

Except…she didn't really understand.

'Why did you decide to travel so far away…to cut yourself off from the rest of your family?' she demanded. 'When Beabea…when the time comes…I'll be completely alone in the world. I'd give anything to know that there were other people who were going to be there for me…uncles and aunts and cousins who would be feeling the same loss when she's not there any more.'

'There are reasons,' he began stiffly.

'I'm sure there are, but why punish yourself unnecessarily?' she demanded, her own heart aching for his loss and wishing she could ease it for him. '*You* didn't set the explosion, so why are *you* feeling guilty and putting yourself in exile? You should be in Xandar, showing those fundamentalists—or whoever it was that did it—that they aren't going to win. You should be organising the rebuilding of the unit for all those children that need it…all the Abirs and Neelas and Jasmines who can't come to a small unit in Cornwall, no matter how good it is.'

Emily believed so passionately in what she was saying that Zayed could almost see sparks flying off her as she took him to task.

She was an amazing woman, so open and generous… and magnificent in her fierceness.

If they had met in another place, another time…another life, he would have done everything in his power to make her his, because with a woman like her at his side there was nothing he couldn't accomplish.

Just look at all the things she managed to cram into each and every day.

Not content with a busy and demanding career, she was arriving early for her shift each day to spend extra time with their little patients so that their bewildered parents would be relaxed enough with her to voice their fears. Then she was hurrying back to Penhally to spend time with her grandmother, often returning several times during the evening to take advantage of the increasingly brief spells between her morphine-induced sleep.

She hadn't even bothered to ask for permission to visit his home after that first time, simply assuming that she would be welcome to join in the nightly mayhem of story time and lingering long enough to give every child a moment or two of gentle attention, playing with them and cuddling them while they settled down for the night so that their parents and carers could have time for a little adult conversation.

And then there was her determination to be present on the beach each evening to watch over him.

He sighed inwardly, still unable to work out how he felt about that insistence.

His male pride wanted to be offended that she was implying that he might be unable to take care of himself, even as his common sense told him that it was taking unnecessary risks to swim alone, no matter that the beach at Penhally was hardly a remote location.

The one emotion that he hadn't allowed himself to examine was the feeling of pleasure that came over him at the thought that she might care enough about him as an individual to be concerned about his safety, and that was crazy.

The last thing he should want was for Emily to grow to care about him, knowing that he couldn't offer her anything in return. He just didn't have it in him any more and she was a person who deserved the best of everything.

So, even though she was sitting on his bed, close enough to touch, close enough to breathe in the sweet musky scent of her body that never completely disappeared even under the tang of sea water, even though he would like nothing more than to pull her into his arms and never let her go, he had to try to keep a professional distance between them, for both their sakes.

But that didn't mean that he could help himself from loving the way she related to every one of the children, and the quietly steadfast way she showed her love and care for her grandmother, even though having to watch her die by inches was devastating her.

The last couple of days he'd even timed his departure from St Piran's so that he could follow her to the hospice, then waited out of sight until she emerged to make her way to the beach with the few stray tears that escaped her steely control already streaking her cheeks.

He'd discovered by accident just how close she was to tears after each visit and wanted to be there for her, but unless she granted it to him, he had no right to intrude on her private misery.

'Zayed?' The uncertain tone in her voice and the shadows that were gathering rapidly in the room were the only things that told him that he'd allowed the silence to stretch between them for far too long.

'I am sorry,' he said. 'Your words made me think and my thoughts took me in many directions...the explosion...the unit...your grandmother.'

'Oh, I forgot!' she exclaimed. 'Beabea asked particularly if you would come to visit her tonight. She seemed fairly insistent but, of course, only if you have the time. It might mean waiting until she wakes up because she's pretty much drifting in and out at the moment, and—'

'Emily, it is all right. I would be honoured to visit her again,' he interrupted with a smile. He enjoyed her grandmother's spiky sense of humour, which even terminal cancer couldn't take away. It didn't matter that he felt wary of the keen way she watched him each time he visited, as though she were dissecting him right to the bone. He wouldn't have been at all surprised if she possessed the facility for reading minds, the way his own grandmother had seemed to.

'When did you want to go?' he asked, relieved to have a chance to draw some sort of a line under their emotionally fraught conversation this evening. He had never spoken of those events to anyone before and the painful experience had left him feeling drained and on edge.

Then there was the danger that the longer he spent in Emily's company, the more likely it would become that he'd make a slip and reveal how he really felt about her. 'We could leave now, if you like,' he offered, hoping he didn't sound too eager.

The expression in those clear green eyes told him that she knew exactly why he was so keen to go, and left him with the uncomfortable feeling that yet again he was guilty of cowardice.

* * *

His first look at her grandmother's face told him that the end was very close and for a moment he wondered whether he ought to excuse himself and leave the room to give the two of them some precious private time together.

Then she opened her eyes and fixed him with a surprisingly alert gaze, almost as if she'd known what he was thinking.

'Come…closer,' she mouthed faintly, beckoning with a single skeletal finger to make the point.

When he would have demurred, directing Emily to stand closer instead, a glimmer of the fire he'd seen so often in her granddaughter's eyes flashed at him, telling him without words that *he* was the one she wanted to talk to first.

She started to speak, but her voice was so insubstantial that he could barely hear it.

Frustrated, she stabbed an imperious finger into the bedclothes, letting him know in no uncertain terms that she wanted him to sit close beside her.

'You…' she breathed when he leaned as close as he could without crowding her, concerned that she was already struggling for breath, even with the assistance of supplemental oxygen. 'You are…a good man,' she declared in a way that forbade him to argue with her, no matter how much he might want to set the record straight. 'You've…been hurt…' she continued laboriously, 'been sad…but it's time…'

'Time?' He knew that Emily hadn't had a chance to tell her grandmother anything of their conversation this evening, and was uncomfortable with the idea that the older woman could tell so much about him. Perhaps she *could* read his mind, but he certainly couldn't read hers.

'Time…to forgive…yourself,' she whispered. 'Time…to go on…with your life.' She fumbled for his hand, her own feeling almost as weightless as a baby bird in his as she trapped his gaze with a fierce intensity that he wouldn't have believed she was still capable of. 'Promise me…' she said. 'You must promise…you will…take care of…my Emily…'

Those simple words sent fear flooding through him, choking him so that he couldn't utter a single word to deny her.

But he couldn't be responsible for taking care of Emily. It wasn't right that she should ask him. He couldn't take care of anyone—he'd already proved that when he'd let Leika and Kashif die.

'Promise me…' she demanded with all the energy she could summon, and suddenly he knew that, no matter how much he wanted to…no matter how much he should…he couldn't refuse what might be her dying wish.

'I promise,' he said, even as despair crept into his soul with the realisation that he had just vowed to do the impossible.

CHAPTER NINE

BEABEA beckoned Emily to her then and, regardless of the fact that it meant she was almost plastered against Zayed's side, she hurried forward and leant as close as she could.

'I...love you...darling girl,' she managed, but Emily could tell that it was becoming harder and harder for her to form the words. She seemed to be so desperately tired that everything was becoming a real struggle.

'I know, Beabea,' she reassured her, stroking the tissue-paper-fine skin on the back of her hand and trying to ignore the unhealthy yellow colour of the jaundice that signalled the severity of her liver failure. 'I've always known. And I love you, too. Now, you get a good night's sleep and we can talk again in the morning.'

She bent to press a kiss to her grandmother's cheek and when she straightened up, she noticed that those faded blue eyes were focusing first on Zayed's face, then on hers.

A sweet smile just lifted the corners of her mouth as she closed her eyes.

'No more...talk...I've said...all that needed...to be said,' she managed with what sounded almost like satisfaction before her hand relaxed its grip in Emily's.

'She's asleep,' Zayed whispered, and Emily realised that her sudden panic must have shown in her face. 'Her heart is still beating,' he pointed out, indicating the pulse still beating at her grandmother's throat. But not for long, was the silent rider that he didn't need to say aloud.

Emily waited until they were outside the hospice wing, standing by their respective cars, before she tackled him about the private conversation he'd had with her grandmother.

'Beabea was speaking so softly that I couldn't hear what she was saying to you,' she said, suddenly realising that she sounded quite stiff with the resentment that he'd taken up some of her precious time with her grandmother. 'What were the two of you talking about?'

Zayed's eyes looked almost black in the shadows this far away from the security lights and his expression was totally unreadable as she waited for him to speak.

Instead, there was a sudden call from the door they'd only recently exited.

'Emily!' called the sister on night duty who had only just wished them goodnight as they'd passed her desk. She beckoned. 'You'd better come in, quickly. Your grandmother's taken a turn for the worse.'

'Beabea!' Emily exclaimed frantically as she whirled and started to run.

It was a short corridor but it felt as if the faster she ran the further away her grandmother's door became until Zayed caught her hand and ran beside her.

Emily wasn't quite sure how he came to be beside her or how she came to be holding his hand so tightly, but she was very aware that having Zayed with her was her only comfort at that moment.

Unfortunately, by the time they hurried through the door they were just in time to see the nurse release her grandmother's wrist with a shake of her head.

'I'm so sorry,' she said, and seemed genuinely upset that the end had come so quickly—just moments after Emily had left her grandmother sleeping peacefully. 'She was a lovely lady.'

Emily's legs refused to hold her for a second and she was even more grateful that Zayed was there willing to lend his strength to lower her safely into the familiar chair at the side of Beabea's bed.

At first glance Beabea didn't look any different to the way she'd been when Emily had glanced back at her from the doorway just minutes ago. But there *was* a difference—in some indefinable way it was obvious that her grandmother just wasn't *there* any more.

Emily had expected to cry bitterly when this moment finally arrived, but she was too stunned for tears, overwhelmingly aware of an enormous feeling of loss and emptiness.

'Emily? You are all right?' Zayed asked gently, his arm tightening supportively around her shoulders. 'Do you want me to drive you home?'

Home? *That* nearly broke through the strangely echoing distance that had appeared between her and the rest of the world.

The little cottage that she'd shared with her grandmother ever since her parents had died was *Beabea's* home, and now that she was gone, it felt to Emily almost as if *she* didn't have a home any more.

'I can't leave yet,' she said in a voice that felt as if it scratched her throat on the way out. 'There are the formalities to see to and…and…'

'Shh,' he soothed, as if he knew she was just seconds away from flying apart into a million pieces. 'First you just need to sit here quietly with your grandmother to say your last farewell.'

He was so understanding of the churning chaos inside her that she only just held onto her control, but the dark shadows in his eyes reminded her that the reason why he knew what she needed was because he had suffered so much worse.

At least Beabea's life had been long and full. Zayed's son had hardly begun to live when his life had been snuffed out like an ephemeral candle flame.

'I'll be fine,' she said, and hoped that the smile she managed looked a little more convincing than it felt. But she had to try. It wasn't fair, after all the sadness he'd suffered, for him to be burdened with her unhappiness, too. It could only bring back the memories that haunted him. 'I expect that someone on the staff here will have telephoned the surgery for someone to certify the death. Once that's over, I'll go home.'

'Are you sure that is what you want? I do not mind waiting with you,' he offered, and sounded as if he really meant it.

She was so tempted to accept, knowing that just to have him by her side would make everything so much more bearable, but Beabea hadn't raised her to be a coward.

'I'm sure,' she said quietly, and he nodded, accepting her decision.

'Ring me on my mobile to tell me when you leave,' he suggested, and when he took that first step away from her she was already wishing she could change her mind, especially when he added, 'If you want me to come over, I will come—so you are not alone.'

'Dr Tremayne's arrived,' Nan Yelland murmured softly, and Emily blinked. She'd completely lost track of time while she'd been sitting there, her mind wandering over so many happy memories in the years since she'd come to live with Beabea.

'What time is it?' she asked, her voice sounding as rusty as if it hadn't been used in a long time.

'Nearly three o'clock,' said a male voice in the doorway.

For just a second her heart leapt with the hope that it would be Zayed standing there, but it was only the very tired and rumpled figure of Nick Tremayne.

Emily smiled at him, feeling a sense of rightness that he should be the one to see Beabea for the last time. He'd been her GP ever since he'd started the practice in Penhally and her grandmother had always had a great deal of faith in him. It just wouldn't have been the same if a stranger had performed this last duty.

'I'm sorry I couldn't get here any earlier, my dear,' he said, as he placed his bag very precisely on the bedside table and released the locks. It only took him a second to find the relevant paperwork. 'There was an accident out at the junction of Penhally View and Dunheved Road. Youngsters going too fast and one didn't make the corner.' He looked up with a wry twist to his mouth. 'You'd think local lads would grow up knowing that you can never win in an argument with a Cornish stone hedge.'

'Was anyone hurt?' Emily seized on the topic to take her mind off the fact that he was treating her grandmother so impersonally. Although he was being perfectly respectful, it seemed almost as if she was no longer a person to him any more, just a routine job to be done.

Did it seem that way simply because he was exhausted at the end of a long, traumatic day or was it perhaps a defence mechanism, his way of dealing with seeing his patients when they were no longer alive, by shutting a part of himself away inside?

Would she ever be able to do that if they lost one of their little charges? Would that be the way she could cope with the feeling that she should have been able to do something more for them?

'The passenger was trapped and it took a while to cut him free,' he continued. 'He'll probably be on crutches for a while when they get his leg reassembled, but the driver was unconscious at the scene—a depressed skull fracture. We'll just have to wait and see what St Piran's can do with him. If it's as bad as it looked, he might never come out of ICU, even if he makes it out of Theatre.'

The sharp click of locks drew her attention to the fact that he'd just closed his oversized briefcase again.

'I've done the necessary,' he said as he turned towards her. 'Of course, you know that there'll be no need for a post-mortem. It wasn't as if her death was unexpected or that the cause is in any doubt.'

'No.' Somehow Emily forced her voice to work. 'Thank you for coming out so late,' she added, the manners that Beabea had always insisted on a totally automatic part of her life even when everything else had been turned on its head.

'Nan told me you were sitting with her and I couldn't leave you here all night.' He reached out an avuncular hand to pat her on the shoulder. 'She was a lovely lady and it was always a pleasure to see her. I'm sure you'll feel better when you've had a good cry, my dear. Just concentrate on the fact that she'd had a good innings— and that she was tremendously proud of you—but if you'd like me to organise some grief counselling...'

'I don't think so,' she said firmly, not seeing the point. No amount of counselling would bring her grand-mother back and she would rather deal with this loss the same way she'd dealt with the loss of her parents—in her own way and in her own time.

Still, it was kind of the man to spare the time to talk to her like this, especially when he must be longing to get back home to his bed. But all Emily could think was that it was wasted on her when she would far rather that it was Zayed comforting her. And it could have been, except she'd been stupid enough to send him away.

'The sky's always darkest just before the dawn,' she could hear Beabea's voice saying as she drove slowly down the driveway, but it seemed as if this night was never going to end in the bright promise of a new day.

She halted at the junction with Mevagissey Road, knowing she ought to turn left to go back to the cottage, but suddenly she couldn't face going there.

There was only one place she could go while her emotions were in such turmoil and that was her secret thinking place on the beach, the hidden nook among the rocks that had played host to almost every decision she'd ever made about her life—whether she really cared at thirteen years of age that stuck-up Melanie Philp didn't want to be her best friend any more; whether to cut her waist-length hair really short before her school leavers'

Ball to make herself look more grown-up and ready for the big wide world; whether to specialise in paediatrics or surgery, and so many other milestones, great and small.

She parked her car at the top of the cliff in the car park near the steps and made her way down to the beach, glad of the thick cardigan she'd grabbed off the back seat. September was going fast and even though the weather was still beautifully warm by day, at this time of the morning, she could feel that autumn was not so far away.

Beabea had always said that autumn was her favourite time of the year, the season that showed the fulfilment of all the promise of spring and the burgeoning of summer in harvests of fruit and vegetables to sustain them through the winter. She'd especially loved the fabulous displays of colour as the deciduous trees began to shut down for their winter rest.

'I'm sorry you missed the leaves turning colour,' she whispered into the breeze, her heart heavy at the thought that she'd never again come home to a kitchen table covered in a display of brilliantly hued leaves that her grandmother had collected on her walk that day. But even though she hated the thought that she was now all alone in the world, she couldn't in all conscience have wanted Beabea to linger long enough to see the leaves one last time, not with the level of medication it had taken at the end to control her pain.

'Emily,' said the voice she most wanted to hear, and she closed her eyes tightly against the imagined sound, wishing it were real and regretting again that she'd sent Zayed away.

Why had it seemed so important that she show the

world that she had the strength to deal with this loss alone? Why couldn't she simply have admitted just how good it would have felt to lean on him and borrow his strength for a little while?

She was sitting here feeling frozen inside, hardly daring to allow herself to imagine what the days and weeks ahead would be like because she was afraid to.

There! She'd admitted it.

It was all very good saying that she'd coped with loss before and had dealt with it, but the last time she'd had Beabea there to hold her while she'd fallen apart and put herself back together. This time she would have no one because she'd sent away the only person she wanted near her.

In fact, she needed him to be with her so much that a moment ago she had even imagined that she'd heard his voice swirling around her in the chill of the early morning breeze.

'Emily?' The sound of those liquid syllables couldn't belong to anyone else, and she opened her eyes to peer eagerly into the darkness, knowing with a sudden leap of joy that Zayed had come to find her. Was there enough light for him to be able to find this place again? Would he be able to find her in the darkness?

'Zayed. I'm here,' she managed with a rusty croak to her voice as tears of relief began to threaten. She couldn't even get to her feet as the events of the last few hours finally overwhelmed her. 'I'm here,' she repeated, but he was already there in front of her, darker than the darkness surrounding them, arms strong and shoulders broad as he wrapped them around her and invited her to rest her head against him.

'Oh, Zayed,' she whimpered as she burrowed into

him, finally knowing that she had found a safe refuge before the storm broke, and with that thought the tears started to fall.

Even as he wondered what on earth he was supposed to say to her, Zayed ignored the brief flash of panic and simply tightened his hold on the sobbing woman in his arms.

There was no sign now of the dedicated young doctor eager to learn everything he could teach her, or of the empathetic young woman who voluntarily spent her time visiting the convalescent children in his house. This was the young girl whose parents were already long gone and who had just lost the only close relative she had left in the world.

When he hadn't been able to wait any longer for her to contact him, he'd driven back to the hospice to discover that her car wasn't there any more. As he'd already established that it wasn't parked at the cottage, there was only one other place he knew to look.

And, just as he'd guessed, she'd been here in her special place, probably doing nothing more than staring blindly out to sea, feeling numb with disbelief that her beloved Beabea had gone.

He pressed his cheek gently to her head, easily able to empathise with her grief even as he drew in the fresh herbal scent of her shampoo mixed with the underlying essence that was pure Emily.

In his head he could admit just how much he was drawn to her…had been drawn to her from the first time he'd caught sight of her.

To have her in his arms like this, even in such devastating circumstances, was almost enough to make him feel whole again—for all the good it could ever do him.

If he were into self-delusion, he might dream that she could be satisfied with someone who would never really be a whole man again, but why would she?

Emily Livingston was a woman with the whole world at her fingertips, talented, intelligent, beautiful and able to take her pick of any man she wanted. It certainly hadn't escaped his notice that she had every single man in the department lusting after her, to say nothing of the less faithful married ones. Not that she paid any of them any attention, far less accepted their invitations.

What chance would a man who wasn't even a countryman of hers have with a woman so quintessentially English?

A sudden smile flicked across his face when he replayed that last thought. It was a good job that he hadn't voiced it aloud or he would have been shot down in flames.

Not English! Cornish! she would have corrected him proudly. *And don't you forget it!*

'I'm sorry,' hiccuped that same voice from somewhere under his chin. 'I didn't mean to blubber all over you.'

'You may *blubber* all you like,' he invited. 'You know it is an important part of the grieving process.' But it seemed as though the storm was beginning to abate.

'Did you?' she asked when she finally broke the silence again.

'Did I what?' Had he missed a part of the conversation while he'd examined...and dismissed...the idea of asking her to accompany him back to his country?

Even if she were to agree to the idea, how long would it be before she realised that she didn't want to stay with a man without honour; the sort of coward who had let his wife and son die without doing a thing to save them; the sort of man who had fled his country and the never-ending nightmares without doing his utmost to bring justice down on the murderers who'd killed his family.

'Did you cry when you grieved?' she asked softly, but the question had all the impact of the original explosion.

It completely short-circuited his thought processes so that he couldn't brush it aside the way he'd done in the past. This time the only thing that came out of his mouth was the raw, unvarnished truth.

'No, I did not cry, because I did not have the right,' he admitted hoarsely. 'How could I play the wronged husband robbed of his family when it was so much my fault that they died?'

He heard the sharp hiss of her indrawn breath and steeled himself to feel her withdraw from him in disgust.

She did pull back a little way but only so that she could glare up at him in the half-light of the early dawn with eyes that reminded him of those of an angry cat.

'So you set the explosion, did you?' she challenged. 'You invited your wife and child to stand there while you detonated it and then you deliberately did nothing to save their lives?'

'No, I did not make the bomb or detonate it,' he said, impatient that she was deliberately misunderstanding him. 'But they died because I did not do anything to save them.'

'Because you yourself were seriously injured,' she

broke in sharply, but he dismissed that argument the
way he always did. He was a doctor with the skill to
save lives, therefore he should have been able to save
his wife and child. 'And has anything been done to
track down the people who perpetrated this atrocity?'
she continued, apparently only too happy to ignore her
own problems by occupying her thoughts with his.

'That would be difficult, considering the ones who
caused it are the ones who would be charged with inves-
tigating it,' he fired back hotly, and could have cursed
aloud at his indiscretion.

'You mean, you *know* who killed them?' she demanded incredulously. 'And they are not in prison?'

He closed his eyes and counted to twenty, then again
backwards to one, but still the only thing that felt right
was to tell her everything—that his was a family di-
vided, with an uncle who had craved power enough
to try to wipe out any opposition, including his own
brother, while conveniently placing the blame on fun-
damentalist extremists.

'Is there any way of proving this?' she asked, and
his heart swelled with unaccustomed elation when he
realised that her outrage was clearly on his behalf—he
could tell that just by looking at her as the sun started
to peep over the horizon.

'Not unless I go back to Xandar and confront him,'
he said. 'And then, only if he didn't arrange to have me
killed before I could do it.'

'But then? Would you be free to stay in Xandar and
set up another department for your little patients?'

'That would be irrelevant because I will not be going
back,' he said firmly, suddenly struck by the realisation that this time it wasn't the situation in Xandar that

was ruling his decision but the fact that going back to take on such a project would mean breaking the promise he'd made to Emily's grandmother.

And if there was one thing he hated doing, it was breaking promises.

He'd been brought up to be an honourable man, and even though his bride had been chosen for him for political reasons, he'd had every intention of laying down his life to protect her and any family they had. So the fact that they'd died while he lived felt like an indelible stain on his character.

Except...would the promise wrung out of him by Emily's grandmother be a way to lessen that stain? If he were to succeed at taking care of the grieving woman in his arms, would he be able to hold his head up again? Would it be the second chance that Emily had spoken of?

The two situations were not in the least similar. Xandar and all its political turmoil was so very different from peaceful Cornwall, and Leika had been the wife chosen for him, while Emily...

He paused in his thoughts, wondering exactly how he should categorise the person who had brought sunshine into his life just by entering it.

If he were being fanciful, he could say that she, too, had been chosen for him, by her grandmother, placed in his care by an unbreakable promise.

And just why did that thought fill him with dismay and set his pulse racing with excitement at the same time?

'I'm dreading going home,' Emily admitted in a small voice still thick with the threat of tears. 'It was bad enough when Beabea moved to the hospice, but at least she was still almost within sight of the cottage. Now…'

'So come to live with me instead,' Zayed heard himself say with a sense of disbelief.

'Live with me…' Emily's heart stood still as those words wrapped around her, then it started beating again at twice the pace.

'You want us to live together?' The suggestion was so unexpected that she was having difficulty believing that she'd heard him correctly.

'Would that be so bad?' he asked. 'You have already said that you do not want to go to your own home and you seem to enjoy yourself at mine.'

'But that's not what you just said,' she pointed out, scared by her bravery but needing to have everything spelt out in words of one syllable. Her heart was involved here, and she'd already had it broken enough times for one lifetime. 'You invited me to live with you, so I need to know whether that was some sort of proposal or…' Emily could feel her cheeks burning with the fear that she was making a monumental fool of herself.

'I should warn you,' she continued without giving him time to reply, 'just because Beabea's gone, it doesn't mean that I'm going to…to drop my standards.'

That didn't mean that she wasn't tempted to, she admitted silently. Zayed was everything she wanted and she'd fallen deeply in love with him in the short time she'd known him, but she could never be happy with anything less than marriage.

Then there was the fact that he was still carrying so much baggage…so much unwarranted guilt.

'Drop your standards?' he repeated with a frown that was easily visible now that the light was strengthening behind the cliff at their backs, making the sea look as if it stretched away from them like a rippled silver sheet all the way to the horizon.

'It wouldn't feel right to move in with a man without the benefit of marriage,' she said, and cringed when she heard how prim and proper she sounded.

He stiffened against her and she had an awful feeling that she knew exactly what he was going to say when he finally broke the uncomfortable silence.

'I am sorry, Emily, but I had not thought to marry again because I have nothing to offer a woman.'

'Nothing to offer?' This time it was her turn to look puzzled as she leant back far enough to focus directly on his face. 'What do you mean, nothing to offer? You're an intelligent, hard-working man who also happens to be extremely good-looking, and you do a difficult job extremely well.'

'Thank you for that testimonial,' he said wryly, 'but there is one thing that can never be changed, no matter how much you might want to.' The harsh tone of his words drew her eyes up to his to see that dreadful empty look return. She wanted to reach up to cradle his cheek in her hand but somehow knew that this was not a time when he would be comfortable accepting gestures of caring.

'The explosion did not just injure my back,' he continued gruffly. 'The surgeons were convinced that the situation would improve but it looks as if the condition is permanent.'

'Condition?' She could feel the tension tightening still further in his body and knew he would rather be up on his feet and striding around on the sand than sitting here among the rocks with an argumentative, weepy woman in his arms.

'I can never have another child,' he said bluntly, the words exploding out of him. 'It appears that some connections from my spine to my...my masculinity...have been damaged.'

'And you think I would only marry a man if he could give me a child?' she exclaimed as she leapt to her feet, uncertain whether to be insulted that he might think that of her or sad that the idea would have occurred to him in the first place. 'I would never even think to do that because, to me, a child is just the *byproduct* of a marriage. A wonderful byproduct, if you are lucky enough, but the most important people in any marriage will always be the two people who make their vows.'

He rose more slowly and she wondered guiltily whether that time spent with her weight pressing down on him might have stressed his injuries and put back his recovery programme. But one look at his expression told her that the ever-present pain in his back was the last thing on his mind.

It was obvious that he had serious reservations about where the two of them went from here, but she refused to be embarrassed about her assumption that he was making some kind of proposal. If she hadn't, they wouldn't be having this conversation and she'd never have learned about the hidden consequences of his injuries.

'We both need time to think about this,' she said firmly, even though she already knew exactly what she wanted. It was desperately sad that he would never be able to have a child of his own, because the more she'd seen of him the more she'd realised that he would have been a perfect father.

But even if it meant she could never have a child of her own, she would count herself lucky if she had Zayed by her side for the rest of her life.

'In the meantime, there's work and plenty of it waiting for us at St Piran's,' she declared.

'Not for you. Not today,' he said with a shake of his head. He held out one lean hand in invitation to accompany him back up the steps to the car park at the top of the cliff.

Emily held back a moment, finding that she was dreading the start of the new day and loath to end this 'time out of time' together.

Behind him, she could see the first of the early-bird surfers paddling out to catch their first wave of the morning, oblivious to the events of the night that had changed her life for ever.

Zayed turned to follow her gaze, watching the first figure leap agilely to its feet to guide the board so that it received the full force of the incoming wave, before he flicked a glance in her direction. 'And you think you could teach me to do that?' he said in tones of disbelief.

'It's possible, even for someone of your great age,' she teased, but the mention of age brought back other memories that spoiled her enjoyment of the tranquil scene.

'What will you do today?' he asked as they climbed the cliff, and the thought that he would soon be going to work while she was condemned to spend the time alone was depressing.

'There are my grandmother's things to deal with,' she said, dreading the task. 'Perhaps if I do it while I'm

still numb from losing her, it won't hurt quite so much.'
And anyway she needed time to get her head straight
and…

'Do you need company for this?' he offered, and she
felt her eyes grow wide with surprise. 'I will be useful
for carrying things, even if I can not make any decisions about the possessions of your grandmother. Only
you can do this.'

'But you need to go to work.' She should have bit-
ten her tongue rather than give him a cast-iron reason
to leave her to it, especially when his suggestion had
made the awful day seem briefly brighter.

'I have left a message at the unit to say that I will be
away for the day,' he said with the calm assurance of a
man who was obviously accustomed to command. How
had she not seen this before? It would have been a giant
clue to the fact that he was something more than an ordinary man who had worked his way up to his current
position at St Piran's.

'They can call me if there is any urgency,' he added,
'but I do not expect that there will be any problems. All
our little ones are stable and the next intake is not due
for a couple more days.'

Reassured that he already had everything organised,
Emily accepted his offer with something suspiciously
like excitement. She found herself glancing into her mir-
ror all the way along Harbour Road to check that he was
following her towards the cottage, and realised she was
behaving with all the sophistication of a smitten teenager.

She'd parked her car and locked it and was walking back to join him by his much more stylish vehicle

when they heard shouting coming from further along the harbour.

'That sounds as if it's coming from somewhere near the surgery,' Emily suggested with a frown as she glanced in that direction. 'We don't usually get drunken disturbances at this time of day…in fact, September is usually a fairly quiet month once the children have all gone back to school. It's unlikely to be anyone hoping to break in for drugs—not in broad daylight.'

She had her keys in her hand ready to unlock the front door when there was a loud bang and a scream. Then they both heard someone shout, 'Fire,' and without a second's hesitation they both began to run.

CHAPTER TEN

'It's Althorp's,' Emily called as soon as they were close enough to work out where the noise and smoke were coming from. 'The boatyard,' she clarified when she remembered that Zayed might not know the names of the various businesses along Harbour Road.

The mental image of the business, mainly constructed of time-weathered timber and probably containing dozens of drums of flammable paints and chemicals needed for the building and refurbishing of boats of all sorts, was enough to make her shudder.

There could be any number of boats in there too, from simple wooden dinghies to cruisers worth hundreds of thousands of pounds. Any fire would spread frighteningly fast with so much combustible material around.

She was beginning to pant by now but even though she was running on the road in unsuitable footwear after a night of no sleep and too much emotion, the adrenaline surging through her system lent wings to her feet.

There had been several more explosions since that first one and as she got closer she could see that the flames were already leaping above roof height and scattering burning embers in all directions.

But her first thought wasn't about the destruction of property, no matter how historic it was to Penhally. She was far more concerned about the possibility that some of the boat-builders might already have started work, and if there were people trapped in that inferno...

Zayed was already silently cursing the fact that that his injuries were slowing him down.

There had been a time when Emily would never have been able to outrun him, but today he had to bear the frustration of watching her gradually pulling away from him as she sprinted towards the heavy smoke that had started billowing out across the road towards the harbour.

And then he was there, right in front of the gaping wooden doors to the yard when the wind momentarily lifted the thick smoke, and it was like looking into the mouth of hell.

Instantly, Zayed was catapulted right back to the explosion that had killed Leika and Kashif and had come close to ending his own life.

For several interminable seconds he was paralysed with remembered terror as he relived the realisation that he couldn't even stretch his hand out far enough to touch them.

Then there was another explosion, louder than all the rest, and the shock wave sent Emily reeling back into him, sending both of them to the ground.

Immediately he was helping her to her feet but when he tried to push her behind him to protect her from the flying debris, she grabbed his arm and pointed at the dark outline of a figure trying to make his way into the yard.

'Dammit, *no*!' she screamed over the roar of the flames that were consuming everything in their path as she leapt forward to grab hold of the figure. 'It's only a bloody boat!'

He reached for the man's other arm before it could land the blow that would force Emily to let go, and suddenly they were both struggling to hang on, fighting to hold onto the smouldering clothing and the powerfully built person inside it to prevent him trying to enter the death trap that the yard had become.

Zayed twisted one of the man's arms up behind his back to help Emily to restrain him from his intention of trying to save his precious boat from the flames.

What he knew he would rather be doing than keeping the ungrateful individual from risking his life was grabbing Emily into his arms and taking her as far away from danger as possible.

'Let me go!' the man roared, his eyes wild as he saw the flames spreading with nightmare speed. 'I'm going to lose everything.'

'A boat can be replaced with money,' Zayed shouted right in the man's face, automatically noting that several blisters had formed down one cheek. 'People cannot!'

'It's not just a boat,' the man argued, fighting like a demon, and for a brief second Zayed wondered if it was worth risking permanent damage to his back to restrain a man intent on such lunacy. 'That's my whole life going up in there,' he continued. 'The yard, the sail loft, other people's boats…'

With the sound of the fire engines arriving, all the fight suddenly went out of him and he allowed Zayed and Emily to direct him to the paramedic already parked a safe distance away on the other side of Penhally Bay Surgery next door.

'Are you all right?' Zayed demanded, as he and Emily were bustled aside to leave the firemen space to get their equipment functioning as quickly as possible.

It was obvious that there wasn't going to be much of Althorp's left to save, even once the powerful hoses started pouring thousands of gallons of water onto the inferno. The blaze had become so fierce so quickly that very little in there had stood a chance, not the buildings or the craft, large or small.

'I'm all right,' Emily reassured him, her eyes fixed in awful fascination on the destruction taking place right in front of them.

They were standing by the far corner of the surgery now, but the heat was still reaching them. Even so, Zayed was confident that the granite that formed the surgery's stone walls was solid enough to be unaffected. The paintwork on the side closest to the fire was another matter. That would probably already be showing evidence of scorching and blistering.

Nick Tremayne was standing just a few feet away, his face creased by a deeply concerned frown. He was probably noting just how much work would need to be done before the winter came, but, considering the ferocity of the fire and its proximity to the surgery, they'd got off very lightly.

The woman who came to join him in his vigil was another matter entirely. With tears streaming down her face, it was clear that she was distraught by the destruction of the yard.

'That's Kate Althorp,' Emily told him quietly. 'Her

husband was a partner in the business before he died in the big storm a few years ago.'

'Oh, Nick, look at it.' Kate was sobbing, oblivious to their attention, and they saw the older man put a consoling arm around her shoulders. 'This was Jem's inheritance, and there's nothing left of it.'

'Shh! Kate, everything will be all right,' Nick said soothingly, as Zayed took a look around to see that the emergency services were now fully in charge of the scene. 'Either the business can be rebuilt with the insurance money or...perhaps you and John would be interested in selling the site to the practice—for parking, initially, but with the new estates going up around Penhally, we'll obviously be needing to expand in the future, take on more staff, perhaps put in a full-time physio. That way, you won't have to worry about money for...for Jem's schooling or...'

His voice and the concern in it faded into the distance as Zayed led Emily away, only realising as he wrapped an arm around her shoulders that both of them were shaking in the aftermath of the event.

'Are you sure you are all right?' he demanded, suddenly realising just how much this woman's safety meant to him. 'You were not hurt when that man—'

'Poor John,' Emily said softly. 'The boatyard has been in his family for years and years.'

'But everyone is out of danger, and the fire will soon be under control, yes?'

Emily was quiet for a moment before she replied, then stopped almost in the middle of the pavement in front of Beabea's cottage to gaze up at him. 'Oh, I hope everyone is all right, Zayed.' She paused for a moment and he could tell from the little frown pulling her brows together that she was trying to decide whether to continue. Or was it a question she wanted to ask?

'Did it bring everything back?' she demanded softly, concern clear in those beautiful green eyes. 'The explosions? It must have been...'

'Yes,' he admitted, remembering his utter paralysis for just those few seconds. 'For a moment it was almost like being back there, at the hospital in Xandar, and I was sure I would not be able to move to help anyone.'

'But you could and you did, because *this* time you weren't one of the injured ones,' she declared firmly, obviously determined to stress the fact that had finally been driven home to him in that moment.

'I know this now,' he admitted, with a new sense of peace spreading through him. 'But I will probably always feel sad that I was not able to do anything for Leika and Kashif, even if I could not have saved their lives.'

'Well, you helped me stop John Althorp from risking his,' she pointed out as she sorted through her key ring for the front door key. 'I couldn't have held him much longer on my own, not when he was so determined to go back into the yard.'

She paused when the door swung open, looking back over her shoulder to ask, 'Are you sure you want to do this? It's mostly going to be a long and boring job and I'm probably going to weep buckets when I come across all the little mementos Beabea kept.'

Zayed stared at this special woman who had come into his life and was suddenly overwhelmed with the knowledge that she was the one person with whom he wanted to spend the rest of his days.

He desperately wanted the chance to spend every one

of those days doing his best to make her happy, even if he couldn't give her the children she deserved. Perhaps she could learn to be content with a constant stream of other people's children to care for.

'Emily, will you marry me?' he asked with his heart in his mouth.

'Wha—what did you say?' she stammered, her eyes wide and a dark forest green as she gazed up at him, clearly every bit as shocked as he was to hear the words he'd just said.

'I said, "Emily, will you marry me?"' he repeated firmly, as a feeling of excitement flooded through him at the knowledge that everything in his life was going to be different from this day on. It was almost a feeling of dizziness mixed with the sensation that that he might float right up off the granite front doorstep at any second, a feeling that, for the first time in his life, the world held endless possibilities.

'Why?' she asked faintly. 'Why do you want to marry me? Is it just because I said I wouldn't live with you? Because if it is…'

'No, Emily!' He felt a smile spreading over his face. 'I respect you for that, but it is not why I am asking you to marry me. I am discovering that, for me, there is really only one reason to propose to a woman and that is because I have fallen in love with her and can not imagine my life without her.'

He was glad to see that the shock was lessening a little but her eyes were still wide with disbelief when he took her in his arms for the second time that day. But this time it wasn't to comfort her as she mourned her grandmother but to kiss the mouth that had been fascinating him for weeks.

* * *

Zayed's mouth was everything she had dreamed it would be and more, and she couldn't help the whimper that escaped when he took it away far too soon.

She needed that close connection to him, now more than ever. When that explosion had knocked them off their feet, she'd suddenly realised just how vulnerable the two of them were, standing in front of that raging inferno, and that Zayed might not be lucky a second time. The thought that she might lose him before she'd ever told him that she loved him had squeezed a tight fist around her heart and stopped the breath in her throat.

In that moment she had recognised the essential truth that, even if he wasn't ready to commit to marriage, she would rather be with him than without him. Even as they were walking back to the cottage, she'd been trying to find the words to tell him that, if he still wanted her to, she was ready to accept his invitation to move in with him.

Except she hadn't needed to compromise her principles, because that same explosion had apparently been an epiphany for Zayed, too, and there in the hallway of her grandmother's cottage, after a sleepless night and smelling of smoke, he'd asked her to marry him.

Suddenly she found herself chuckling at the incongruousness of the setting.

'You think it is funny that I ask you to marry me?' Zayed demanded, trying to sound outraged, but her response to his kiss must already have told him what her answer would be.

'I think it's wonderful that you've asked me,' she reassured him. 'I was only laughing because Penhally is surrounded by some of the most beautiful scenery in the world and you chose the hallway of my grand-mother's cottage to propose.'

'So, what would you prefer?' he challenged. 'For me to take you out for a perfect meal first? Or perhaps I should put you in the car and take you further along the coast to find some sand dunes, then put up a Cornish version of a Bedouin tent so that I can ask you properly?'

Emily was laughing out loud now, the happiness bubbling out of her, but Zayed hadn't finished.

'How about if I promise to take you out into the desert when we go to visit Xandar and propose to you properly?' he suggested, his eyes very dark and solemn, and her laughter quickly died away.

'You're serious?' she demanded, knowing just what a huge step this was for him. 'You're really going back to visit Xandar?'

'Initially, it would be a visit, but only if you will be coming with me,' he said firmly. 'Then, when I have put the evidence in front of those who will deal with the one who I believe was ultimately responsible for the death of my wife and son, perhaps we can start to make plans for a new hospital unit for the little ones... but only if you decide you would like to live in Xandar.'

'Ah, Zayed,' she breathed, loving him all the more for the way he was going to face his demons, but before she could accept his proposal he was speaking again.

'Do not give me an answer now,' he said, with a fierce light of excitement filling his dark eyes with sparks of golden fire. 'Wait until we are in Xandar. You will come with me to my country?'

'Of course I'll come with you,' she agreed, loving this new facet to his character. She didn't need elaborate, romantic scene-setting to tell him that she loved him and wanted to accept his proposal. Neither did she need to see Xandar to know that if she was with him she would love it, too, especially if they were going to be working on those plans together.

His eyes lit up and he tugged her back into his arms. 'Ah, we have so much to do today, Emily,' he said, full of bubbling enthusiasm. 'We must decide what to do about the things of your grandmother, make arrangements for someone to take our places in the unit, and then contact my friends in Xandar to prepare them for our visit. But first I need one more kiss before we start to work.'

'Where are we going?' Emily demanded as her horse followed Zayed's out into the apparently endless sand dunes.

'Not much further,' he promised, his accent more pronounced than ever since they'd arrived in his homeland.

'You said that five minutes ago,' she reminded him, but she didn't really mind how long the journey took. This was like something out of a fantasy. Just two weeks ago they'd been in Penhally, feeling the heat of the fire as Althorp's yard had burnt to the ground. Today she was swathed in fine white cotton to ward off the heat of the burning desert sun in Xandar.

And then they rounded the curve of a dune and she knew exactly where he'd brought her and why.

'A Bedouin tent?' she asked with a tremulous smile as he lifted her off the pretty little mare.

'The Xandar equivalent,' he admitted, as he held out a hand to help her dismount and invite her into the shady interior. 'If you would like to make yourself comfortable, I will bring you something to eat and drink.'

In a move that had quickly become automatic, Emily stepped out of her shoes by the doorway and trod across a thick, smooth richly patterned carpet that could only be made of silk.

The cushions piled around the low table were covered in silk, too, and in every opulent lustrous shade imaginable.

'Do I sit on them or lie down?' she murmured uncertainly to herself.

'Whichever you prefer,' he said softly from right behind her as he relieved her of the voluminous robe that had protected her from the heat. Underneath she wore a simple garment, a gift from Zayed in the finest silk, that drifted and clung to her body with the slightest breeze.

When she'd donned it, she'd been almost embarrassed by how much it revealed, but here, alone with Zayed and seeing the gleam it brought to his eyes, it seemed to bring out the sensual side to her nature.

'Would you like something to eat…some fruit, perhaps? Or can I get you a drink?'

Either would have been lovely, but in spite of the fact that he'd obviously enjoyed himself creating the romantic fantasy he'd described on the day of the fire in Penhally, she could tell that he had something else on his mind.

For just a second she allowed insecurity to persuade her that he was regretting bringing her to Xandar, but she knew that wasn't true.

In fact, just today he'd been overjoyed to tell her that the uncle who had been so hungry for power that he had tried to engineer the death of Zayed's entire family had finally been arrested and imprisoned, and was awaiting trial.

'Zayed, what's the matter?' she asked. 'Is there a problem with setting up the replacement unit at the hospital?'

His immediate smile was reassurance enough.

'Not at all,' he declared confidently. 'Everything is going to plan without a hitch since the Hananis and their influential family got together with some of the other parents to tell everyone about what we've done for their children.'

He sank slightly gingerly onto the pile of cushions beside her and she wondered if she ought to suggest massaging his back to relieve the stiffness. It would probably take a while before his body became accustomed to riding again, but she had every confidence that he would eventually regain most of his mobility.

'Emily, even the most hard line of the traditionalists were won over by all those successful operations, and especially by all the good things the families had to say about my new colleague, despite the fact that she is a woman. They have made it a source of national pride that as soon as the unit is completed, these operations will all be able to take place in Xandar from now on.'

My new colleague. There was something almost possessive about the way he'd said those words that had sent a shiver of joy through her, but she couldn't ignore the shadow she'd seen in his eyes.

'So what *is* the problem?' she pressed, knowing that neither of them would be able to relax and enjoy this romantic idyll until they'd discussed whatever it was.

'While you were getting ready to ride with me, I

caught an item on the international news,' he said reluctantly.

'And?' she prompted with a slight frown, wondering what sort of news would put that concerned expression in those gold-shot dark eyes.

'It seems that when we left Cornwall, the beautiful weather did not last. There were pictures showing that there has been a flash flood in Penhally.'

'A flood? In Penhally, itself? Was anybody hurt?' The images of all the people she knew in the town, friends and neighbours right from the first day she'd come to live with her grandmother, flickered before her eyes. 'How much damage was done?'

'I did not hear anything about any injuries, but I did see…' He hesitated briefly before continuing. 'I am sorry, Emily, but I recognised it from the pictures taken from the helicopters. The house of your grandmother was one of those that were flooded.'

'Oh, no!' Emily felt the hot press of tears burning her eyes at the thought that a lifetime's memories had probably been washed away in a matter of seconds.

None of her belongings would have been damaged because they'd all been removed and put in temporary storage before she and Zayed had left for Xandar. But the house itself, with its solid stone walls and Delabole slate roof and the ancient floorboards polished over the decades to a lustrous dark honey colour, to say nothing of all the memories attached to every nook and cranny… all that could have been destroyed in the blink of an eye.

And then there would be the aftermath.

She'd seen enough of what had happened after the Boscastle and Crackington Haven floods at first hand to know that by the time the flood damage had been cleared and the repairs had been completed, it would seem like a completely different cottage.

For a moment it felt as if a hand squeezed tightly around her heart when she realised that, with her job at St Piran's ably filled by one of Zayed's colleagues, there would now be nothing left to go back to in Penhally.

But, then, why would she want to go back there when everything she wanted was here in Xandar?

'Zayed, it's all right,' she reassured him, reaching up a hand to cup his cheek. 'It's always sad when something is destroyed, but it's only a house several thousand miles away. And as you said when the boatyard went up in flames, it can be replaced with money if I ever wanted to go back to Penhally. It's people that are important, people that are irreplaceable.'

'You are certainly irreplaceable,' he said seriously as he knelt beside her, and she suddenly realised that the moment she'd been waiting for had come. 'You have become the other half of my soul, Emily Livingston, and now that I have brought you out into the desert in the country of my birth, it is time for you to give me your answer. Will you marry me so that my soul can be whole again?'

'Oh, Zayed, yes! Of course I'll marry you,' she said as she held her arms out towards him. 'You're the other half of my soul, too, and I'll need you for the rest of my life.'

'Ah, Emily, my Emily,' he murmured as he took her in his arms and their lips met for the first time since he'd kissed her in the hallway of Beabea's cottage.

Their kisses quickly became heated after their self-imposed abstinence and Emily had no objection when Zayed began to explore the willing body beneath the garment he'd given her. How could she when she was equally eager to explore the smooth skin and taut muscles of the body she hadn't touched since that night on the beach in Penhally?

Suddenly Zayed rolled away from her, putting far too many brightly coloured cushions between them as he gazed at her in a strange mixture of disbelief and hope.

'What's the matter, Zayed? Did I do something wrong?' She felt the heat of a blush sweep up her throat and into her face. 'I'm afraid I haven't had very much experience at this sort of thing, so you'll have to tell me what you—'

'Ah, Emily, my Emily, I love your innocence. It will almost be a shame to destroy it, but...' He rolled back towards her again and took her hand in his.

'Since we have been kissing and I have been exploring your body, I have made the discovery that my surgeon did not know everything,' he said with a gleam in his eyes. 'He did not know that when my Emily accepted my proposal and kissed me, she would revive the part of me that the doctors could not.'

Emily's blush grew fiercer still when she followed his downward glance and realised what he was talking about, but she quickly decided that this was no time for maidenly modesty.

'Hmm. This could be a problem,' she said seriously, and had to stifle a laugh when Zayed's face fell.

'A problem?' he echoed uncertainly.

'Well, we aren't married yet, so Beabea wouldn't approve if we were to...take advantage of the situation. But...' She deliberately drew the word out, loving the fact that this powerful man was completely in her thrall for the moment.

'But?' he prompted, completely unable to hide his eagerness.

'But just in case there's the slightest chance that your doctors were right and this may never happen again,' she suggested, 'perhaps...'

'Perhaps?' he pressed impatiently and she marvelled at his control. She was also looking forward to the moment when that control broke.

This, she realised with a burgeoning sense of her own power as a woman, *this* could be the most wonderful game between them, and it was one that could have as many variations as there were hours to their lives.

'Perhaps we ought to take advantage of it while we can?' she hinted, and finally lost control of the happy smile she'd been hiding.

'Ah-h! I was not expecting this to happen, so I have brought nothing with me to protect you,' he groaned, holding back when all she was longing for was to finally learn what it was to be completely possessed by the man she loved. It was something that she'd believed his injuries had robbed them of and she thought she'd schooled herself to accept that this would never happen, but she'd never thought that they would be this fortunate.

'I don't need to be protected,' she told him eagerly, as a quick mental calculation of dates sent an arrow of excitement through her.

She'd been teasing him, but they both knew that there was very little likelihood that his prowess would only have returned for this one occasion. Still, could they really be so lucky as to conceive a child in the first time they came together?

'I would never need to be protected from you,' she

whispered as she raised her arms to allow him to slide her silky covering away, feeling powerful and womanly when she saw the gleam in his eyes as they travelled over her nakedness for the first time. 'I just need to know that I have your love as you have mine.'

'Ah, my Emily, you have it,' he said. 'You have my love, my heart, my soul and my body...for ever!' And he made them one.

* * * * *